11/20

S0-BBS-398

Praise for Jennifer Strange

"JENNIFER STRANGE is a gruesomely fun, demon-infested YA romp in which two teenage sisters learn and ply the family's secret demon-fighting trade. A promising debut."
–**Paul Tremblay**, author of *A Head Full of Ghosts* and *Survivor Song*

"Plenty to appeal to readers: the illustrations that help to visualize the creatures and describe the charms that protect the girls, and two determined young women who awaken to their new powers....As a first novel introducing new characters, readers can hopefully look forward to a deepening of those story lines."
–**School Library Journal**

"This debut novel is overflowing with sardonic wit and memorably feisty (and satisfyingly angry) female protagonists. Jennifer and her sister Liz are unbowed by the gruesome might of their powers, and they adapt as quickly as possible to learning how to use them to keep the gate between the living and the dead closed. Occasional illustrations and journal entries add context, with the highlights being the handful of creepy drawings of monsters Jennifer and Liz face during an eventful few days. It's clear this is a story that has more to come, and horror buffs will happily anticipate the next volume."
–**The Bulletin of the Center for Children's Books**

"Devilishly paced and drenched in Gothic atmosphere, JENNIFER STRANGE is a wild, spine-tingling ride."
–**Claire Legrand**, New York Times-bestselling author of *Furyborn* and *Sawkill Girls*

"A mysterious, dark, and perfectly bone-chilling tale of self-discovery and seizing your destiny, Jennifer Strange is a tremendous addition to young adult horror. Breathtaking illustrations and gruesome descriptions mix beautifully with a story that manages to pull on your heartstrings and terrify you at the same time. I couldn't recommend it more."
–**Amy Lukavics**, author of *Daughters unto Devils* and *The Ravenous*

"What if ghosts and demons really did walk among us (and who's to say they don't?)—Jennifer Strange takes readers deep into a world beyond the one we think we know; a world of magic, talismans, sigils, dark beings and ancient prophesies. Prepare to be delighted and terrified as you get swept away in Cat Scully's spellbinding debut."
–**Jennifer McMahon**, New York Times-bestselling author of *The Winter People* and *The Invited*

"Cat Scully has a wickedly dark streak and talent to spare. JENNIFER STRANGE is a wonderfully creepy southern gothic full of ghosts, magic, and dreadful family secrets, all stewed in the sultry swelter of haunted Savannah, Georgia. This book ticks all the boxes for me, and Scully weaves it all together beautifully!"
–**Christopher Golden**, New York Times bestselling author of *Ararat* and *Snowblind*

"Jennifer Strange comes on like a freight train filled with the screaming corpses of a thousand nightmares, fast paced and unrelenting. I didn't like it, I loved it. It's nice to see someone who remembers that horror should be scary! Catherine Scully doesn't just tell a good tale, she drags you into her world and shoves you into the dark places where the monsters hide. A phenomenal first book!"

–**James A. Moore**, author of the *Seven Forges Series* and *The Last Sacrifice*

"Cat Scully's debut, JENNIFER STRANGE, wastes no space showing you exactly what you're in for. The first time I started this novel, my reaction was, 'THIS is a YA book?!' HELL yeah, it is. But it ain't just kids' stuff. Scully doesn't pander or soft pedal a story about young people facing their demons. She's written a mature, compelling horror story with heart and real scares straight from jump. Take note of Scully's name, folks. She's here to raise Hell, in a really good way. JENNIFER STRANGE is proof of that."

–**Bracken MacLeod**, Bram Stoker and Shirley Jackson Award-nominated author of *Mountain Home* and *Closing Costs*

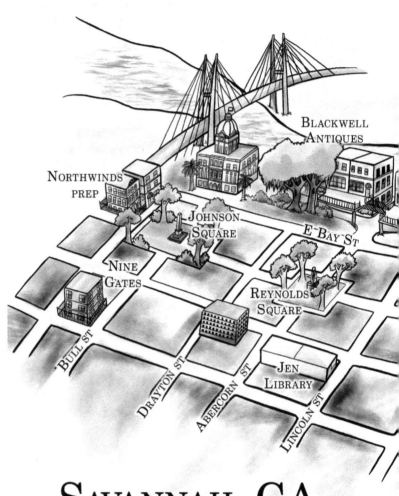

NORTHWINDS PREP

BLACKWELL ANTIQUES

JOHNSON SQUARE

E. BAY ST

NINE GATES

REYNOLDS SQUARE

BULL ST

DRAYTON ST

ABERCORN ST

JEN LIBRARY

LINCOLN ST

SAVANNAH, GA

BONAVENTURE
CEMETERY

Written and Illustrated by
Cat Scully

YAP Books
An imprint of
Haverhill House Publishing

This is a work of fiction. Names, characters, places, and incidents are either a product of the authors' imagination or are used fictitiously. Any resemblance to actual events, locales, or persons, living or dead, is entirely coincidental.

Jennifer Strange
© 2020 Cat Scully

Artwork © Cat Scully
Photo © Annie Spratt
Photo © Siora Photography
Book design by Errick Nunnally

Hardcover ISBN: 978-1-949140-05-7
Trade Paperback ISBN: 978-1-949140-06-4

All rights reserved.
Young Adult

YAP Books
Haverhill House Publishing
643 E Broadway
Haverhill MA 01830-2420
www.haverhillhouse.com

To Craig and Katie,
twin stars guiding me home

"The sparrow, however, is regarded as a bird of survival, representing the ability to assert one's desires and place in society. They are symbolic of understanding our place in the world. Sparrows teach us dignity and humility, compassion and charity, for those who have not. They are the personification of humble, self-sacrificing love. It is also a common superstition that sparrows carry the souls to the afterlife."

I found this passage during my studies. It's the closest I can come to describing what you are.

Jennifer, my Jacks, I hope this journal helps you see where I have been to help you understand where you are going.

Love, Dad

1

Uprooted

"DAMN. I RUINED BREAKFAST." Liz slammed the frying pan into the kitchen sink, sending hot, burnt eggs flying across the countertop.

"You didn't have to go all out," I said. "I was perfectly fine with Pop-Tarts."

"Forget it." She didn't bother to pick up the eggs. Instead, she grabbed two pairs of metallic sleeves from the pantry and took the seat opposite me at her tiny, round kitchen table. We sat together in her apartment, the smallest listing on the planet, and I found myself questioning all my life choices as my older sister shoved one of the space-age wrappers at me. I took the strawberry-frosted cardboard package and attempted to crack a smile that she did not return. *So much for family reunions.*

I unwrapped my package and chewed as slowly as possible as I watched Liz rip the silver foil off her packet with such force one of the Pop-Tarts went flying. A laugh bubbled up, but I shoved it right back down. *No sudden movements. Don't anger the beast.* She picked up the rejected tart and ate it off the floor anyway.

When Dad said this would be good sisterly bonding time, watching my sister rage-cook me breakfast was not what I had in mind. I pictured us watching a movie together, talking about college or crushes or binging the latest Netflix show, but not Liz's constant shade in my general direction. It's not like I wanted to be stranded in her apartment for a chunk of my freshman year. It's not as if Dad asked my opinion when he decided to drop me off at her apartment in the middle of the rain last night.

I chewed and swallowed the rest of the first Pop-Tart. "So, you're cool about me crashing here, right?"

She flung open her laptop. "Why wouldn't I be?"

Yikes. Better try something else. "Do you have a lot of homework at SCAD?"

She didn't reply. She typed something furiously on her computer as a form of a reply. As I endured her repeat performance of "talking-but-not-talking," it was clear I was crashing on her precious college life at the mega elite Savannah College of Art and Design. It's not like the situation wasn't completely interrupting my life too—new city with no friends, no idea where anything was, and worst of all, no volleyball team.

I rolled my eyes and started into my second tart. "Sure. Type away. Ignoring me will totally solve all of your problems. It's like I won't even be here if you pretend long and hard enough."

She shut her laptop and glared at me so hard I thought my body would spontaneously combust. It was the first time Liz had looked at me for any length of time since she opened the door and found me standing there.

"It's not that I don't want you here," she said. "I'm happy to see you."

I crumbled the empty Pop-Tarts wrapper into a shiny, round ball. "Could have fooled me."

"Contrary to what you might believe," she said. "College isn't like high school. If I miss an assignment, if I'm late to class, if I turn in sub-par work, I'll lose my scholarship. And if I lose my scholarship, I'll be facing ungodly mountains of student debt. But I don't blame you. I blame Dad."

She slammed her laptop into her bag with a growl. "God, this is just so typical of him. Running off because he has to do some random journalism research for his university and leaving you here with me without a time frame. He doesn't seem to grasp the concept that this is my first year at SCAD or your first year of high school. No. None of that matters."

God, I was tired of her treating me like I was twelve, like I had no inkling of how hard college could be. When I woke up this morning in her spare bedroom, I felt super guilty. I was about to blurt out the truth over breakfast, tell her Dad didn't leave me here because of a "research sabbatical." I was going to explain that he's not who he says he is and, really, I'm not who she thinks I am, but now I'm thinking about telling her exactly jack.

At times like these when my sister's behavior burns me up, this super annoying voice pops in the back of my head, and it's my mother reminding me to be nice. *"Don't say something you can't take back."*

Thanks, Mom. Thanks ever so much.

I touched the pink stone on Mom's old necklace, a rose quartz crystal that rested on my collar bone at the end of a gold chain. Dad said it should hide me temporarily, but for how long? He made me promise to keep Liz out of it, but how on earth was I supposed to do that? I had no idea what I was doing or how her necklace supposedly works. He's not right about everything.

I let out my most obvious sigh. "Liz, there's something I have to tell you."

But she wasn't paying attention to me anymore. While I'd been debating what to do, she had already packed up her bag with her laptop and sketchbook and was halfway out the door.

"Liz, seriously," I said. "It's important."

"God, I'm so late," she groaned. "Just Google where your school is. I don't have time to do it for you. Besides, it's only two blocks away; you can't miss it. Uniform is on the sofa. My last class gets out at four."

I got up from my chair. "No, really. We need to talk now, and it has to do with Dad and why I'm here—"

That last bit got her attention, but she quickly shook it away. "Just tell me at dinner, Jacks," she said and slammed the door behind her. The coats hanging on the back of the door swung back and forth from the force of her departure.

Well that went extraordinarily terrible.

I glanced toward the spare bedroom that was now my room, where the trash fire that was my new uniform waited for me. I couldn't believe I was forced to wear something so heinous because Dad had enrolled me at a local charter school. Northwinds Academy. God, it sounded like daycare for rich people, not a school for kids who preferred solving equations to pretty much any other social activity.

Oh yeah. There were still burnt eggs all over the counter and pile of dirty dishes in the sink. I had no idea what Liz wanted me to do with them. Back home, I was the unofficial chore person. Dad was incredibly intelligent but also completely hapless at home maintenance, which meant after Mom died, the house exploded. It seemed like Liz had a similar system going on. She has always been like him, but if I ever told her that, she'd probably burn me alive and then dance in my ashes. Best to leave the mess alone.

I left the kitchen table and headed into my bedroom to further inspect the outfit from hell. Dad didn't give me much time to grab things to decorate, so it was really my starry bed set and constellation night light that made it look anything like home. The navy suit lay there on my bedspread, looking so innocent as it blended into the pattern on the duvet cover. Time to tame the beast.

Nope. The uniform was so much worse on. The black-and-blue plaid skirt hung off my waist like a trash bag. The cut went well past my knees to hide most of my legs while the white button-up shirt itched like someone washed it with a cactus. The stuffy little jacket even came with an embroidered school crest with dual horses rearing.

This was it. This was my life now.

Goddammit Dad.

I grabbed my lunch and my canvas book bag and was about to walk out the door when I remembered Dad's journal. *Damn.* It's still in my room. I grumbled the entire ten-foot trek from the front door to my room. The journal sat alone on my nightstand. The thing was massive and could rival a Stephen King hardcover and was bound in brown leather with a belt buckle across the front that shut with a clasp. It held all of Dad's secrets, all of Mom's art. I picked it up, remembering the one instruction he gave me before he left:

"*Read this, and you'll understand. I wrote the entries; your mother drew the pages. We've wanted to tell you for so long. I'm sorry we waited until now. I'll regret it for the rest of my life that we didn't tell you sooner, but now that you've awakened, you need to know what's coming. Hopefully, I can find what we need before they find you, but if they do come, everything you need to hold them off is right here.*"

I unclasped the belt loop and stopped. *The wound's too fresh.* Last night, I tried to read it, but I couldn't bring myself to get past the first page. I should leave it here, keep it safe. Some prick might steal it on my first day, or worse, a teacher might confiscate it. But leave it here? I wasn't comfortable with that choice either. Liz might come back and find the journal. How would I ever explain? There were sigils and wards, enough that it appeared to be a spell book of some kind. Maybe it would come in handy if the necklace failed. I stuffed it in my backpack, crossed the apartment to the front door, and headed outside.

A fresh wave of humidity smacked me in the face. I staggered down the steps to the parking lot below, feeling like I'd just been sucker punched by the weather. I was panting by the time I reached the sidewalk. The South was notorious for its heat waves, sure, but this put the stupidly named "Hotlanta" to shame.

I turned out of Nine Gates apartments and ducked into a crowd of people who didn't seem to

JENNIFER STRANGE

be sweating at all. How was that even possible? There was no way I would make it to school without sweating right through my uniform. I was going to be the new, sweat-drenched, pit-stained girl at school. Fantastic.

I pushed through the mix of locals and tourists that filled the narrow sidewalk. In Atlanta, we drove absolutely everywhere—to the grocery store, to our friend's house, to the mall. Here, everything was so condensed. I could walk anywhere I wanted—go to the grocery store, see a movie, buy Doritos. The last twenty-four hours had been such hell, I hadn't considered the possibility that moving to Savannah could actually be...*nice*. As I passed beneath the hanging moss and the manicured gardens surrounding stone fountains that belonged on the back of a postcard, the idea of unchecked freedom was nice, but I wasn't elated.

After losing Mom two years ago, I hadn't pictured being happy, living a normal life. The grief had almost swallowed me whole, but in the past couple of months, some amount of happiness had come back whenever I played volleyball with my friends. So much for that. I don't think I could ever show my face in Atlanta again after what my school saw. Everything I'd ever known, and that inch of happiness I'd stolen, it was all gone in just one day. It's hard to believe the attack in the gym was only yesterday.

I checked my phone. My GPS told me to head

8

down the hill in the direction of the main street. I'd been to Savannah before, back when Liz was first considering SCAD for college. Dad took us around the city, but I didn't remember the trip in any detail. At least Savannah was laid out on a grid system that made sense, versus Atlanta where the streets looped in on themselves. One wrong turn there and you were dropped right back where you started.

The breeze carried up from the river and rustled the moss overhead. Cajun spice wafted up from River Street and my mouth watered. We couldn't get quality seafood back home, so the smell hanging under the oak branches was absolutely killing me. Maybe I could guilt Liz into taking me there later for dinner.

I rounded a corner and my map beeped that I was close to the school. Squished between a café and a local bookstore, the ivy and flaking ironwork of Northwinds loomed in front of Johnson Square. The school looked like any other building downtown, around three stories high and made with Georgia clay red brick, but the school crest plastered over everything made it stand out. Every white column and glass window glittered with tradition, heritage, prestige.

What the actual hell, Dad?

This was not a charter school for teens who liked math. It was absolutely a prep school for rich kids. They would figure out I wasn't like them and then the whole school would shun me. How did he get me registered at a place like this with a uniform and everything in less than twenty-four hours? He planned this. There was no way he didn't plan this, but then that would mean he knew what was coming. He knew what would happen to me at volleyball practice yesterday. He knew my power would wake up. I needed to read his journal and I needed to read it now.

I spotted an empty area under a tree in the small courtyard and moved to blend in with a group of students. We passed under a pair of rearing bronze horses that crested the open gate. Inside, there were perfectly manicured hedges and bushes with little pink flowers, oak trees with moss dripping from their branches, and a stone fountain with a single horse rearing at the center. The school's logo was on everything everywhere, even carved into the wood of the giant front doors. This place sure had a thing for school spirit, and it loved to show off how much money the parents poured into it. How very Southern.

Students of all ages surrounded the steps, talking in very distinct groups. A small group of elementary school kids huddled on the steps, high schoolers leaned against the wall on the far side hiding their cigarettes, and middle schoolers laughed as they gossiped around the fountain. *Great.* They all knew each other, had probably been best friends since kindergarten, and now there was no way in. I wanted to pass inside unnoticed, but nope. My red hair had always made it impossibly difficult to hide. With this navy uniform and white shirt, I probably looked like a parade float on the Fourth of July. I put my hand to the side of my face and tried to skirt around the students and make a beeline for the empty bench. A group of middle schoolers stopped talking as I passed, and so did the high schoolers, all of them. Time for plan B—crawl inside a bush and live there the rest of the school year. I could forage for snacks when no one is looking. It will be fine. I could survive for months on that plan.

The bell rang, turning everyone's attention away from me. I wanted to fall down and die with relief, but a girl with the longest black hair I'd ever seen flashed a smile at me. Oh good. The extraordinarily gorgeous girl noticed me. This day was going to crash and burn into a spectacularly epic fireball. I tucked a strand behind my ear and waved too hard, like how a seal slaps when it's happy. The beautiful girl started to walk over to me, but the second bell rang, and she turned away and headed inside with her friends. Damn. So close to potential friendship. I grabbed the rose quartz and thought-prayed as hard as I could.

Please, anybody upstairs who might be listening, please let Mom's crystal work. Let me have some semblance of a normal life again. Let me make one friend.

I took a deep breath and headed inside.

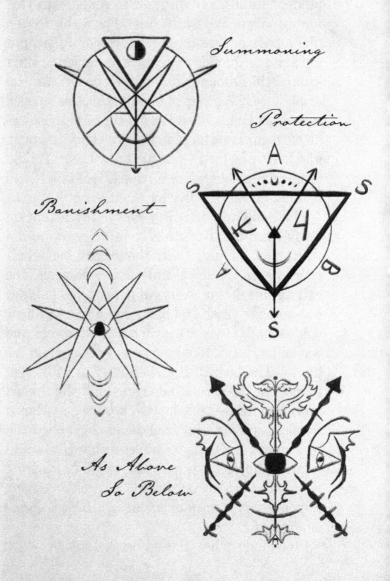

Summoning

Protection

Banishment

*As Above
So Below*

The first thing you need to know about me is that I've lied to you and your sister for most of your lives. My name is Jacob Strange, and I am a demon hunter that grew up in a family of demon and ghost hunters. Once we reached a certain age, we were sent away to another family to study. That's where I met your mother, where I saved her.

In the beginning, Emily and I didn't have much except each other. We fought things using power we didn't understand with no set amount of information to go by on the history of the Sparrows. We wrote down everything in these pages. We learned as much as we could about the possessed, the haunted, the damned and why they wanted your mother's power so badly. The more we traveled, the more we came to realize the awfulness of the truth. Her abilities were far worse than we imagined.

This is not your fault.

Whatever happens, please know it's not your fault. This is because I stole your mother away before we had answers. I hope when you read my journal, you will understand why I had to save her.

I loved your mother more than anything.

Please remember that.

Please know how much I love you.

I hope you will forgive me.

Love, Dad
P.S. These sigils will come in handy. They can be drawn on stones, clothing, or walls. use them and protect yourself.

2

Relations

THE INSIDE OF NORTHWINDS was even worse. It was like a college campus but in miniature. The classrooms, administration offices, and library were scrunched into matchbox space of what used to be a hotel or maybe an office building. Paintings of mountain landscapes and trees hung every five feet in gold or silver frames. The walls alternated between brick or exposed wood. Wow, this place was *loaded*. There was nothing about the school that made me feel comfortable or welcomed or like I belonged at all. Thanks, Dad. As if I wasn't already feeling like I didn't belong back home, now you've sent me to a place that is even worse. At least one thing about it made me feel somewhat okay. Northwinds had a smoky cedar smell, like a campfire burning in deep winter, and that alone put me a little more at ease.

I headed through the glass doors of the administration office. The woman behind the counter was wearing the tightest blazer I'd ever seen. When I asked for my class schedule, she looked me up and down once, and then sniffed like she'd found me on the bottom of her shoe. She handed me a beautifully typed list of classes on a cream-colored cardstock. I resisted thanking her for the wedding invitation. How on earth could Dad afford this? Most of the time our pantry was so bare I had to remind him to buy groceries.

The bell rang and the students emptied out the hallways in seconds. Crap. I was about to miss my first class. My footsteps echoed as I ran, trying to figure out which hall was the correct letter and which classrooms were numbered but it was super confusing. Damnit.

Heeled shoes clacked up the steps as a student ran up the stairs at the end of the hall. Oh. Right. There are levels to this school. Everything isn't all on the first floor like back home. *Good one, Jennifer.* I didn't realize I'd actually face-palmed in real life until I turned around to find two students staring at me. I smiled and scuttled away to the second floor like the embarrassed crab I was.

Room 2C wasn't hard to find. Once I got there, I was clearly in the right place for first period

Biology. Posters about the periodic table lined the walls and every desk had neat sets of beakers and matching Bunsen burners, but part of me doubted my navigational skills because in a room made for twenty, there were only eight students. Back home, classrooms usually held at least twenty students, sometimes thirty. Where in the heck is everybody? Most everyone occupied the first two rows, save for one boy in the back row. He had messy curls and his school shirt unbuttoned down enough for a red t-shirt to peek through, all things that screamed "I don't care about this school or its rules." He looked up last. When we locked eyes, my heart twinged with recognition. I had never hated someone on sight before, but when his eyebrow raised at me and his lip curled a little, I felt justified that everything inside of me physically recoiled.

"Hey, new girl," said a female voice to my right.

The casual way she said it startled me, quelling whatever weird anger had started burning inside my chest. It was the gorgeous girl from the courtyard. Her hair rippled over her shoulder like a small waterfall as she got to her feet and my face became ten thousand shades of red.

She held a hand out to me with white nail polished fingernails. "I'm Ashley Gerard."

You've come this far, I told myself. *Smile. DO NOT vomit on her shoes.*

"I'm Jennifer," I said. "Jennifer Strange."

"Whoa. That's seriously your name?" she said.

"You're like a superhero!"

I laughed a little too loudly, like I had just swallowed a monkey. "Hardly. That's just the name my parents gave me."

I couldn't stop thinking about how perfect her winged eyeliner was. Why was I like this?

She smiled and it was like her face was made of sunshine. "Want to sit next to me?"

"Sure, yeah. That would be great," I said and rolled my backpack off my shoulder onto the black countertop next to her. The butterflies in my stomach would not stop.

She slid back onto her barstool. "Where are you from, Miss Superhero?"

When you're introduced to someone new in Atlanta, the first thing they asked you was: "What do your parents do for a living?" It seemed the first thing people asked you in Savannah was: "Where do you come from?" That's Southern speak for: "Who are your relations?"

"Atlanta," I muttered, and was determined not to say anything else because that information alone was going to cause a stir.

Both of Ashley's eyebrows raised, and it piqued the interest of the girl in the next row.

"What's an *Atlanta* girl doing here?" said the girl with fringe bangs and big pink glasses. Pink seemed to be her signature color, as she also had pink streaks throughout her sleek black bob, which she loved to toss every time she spoke. "Had too much of the big city?"

My neck turned hot. "Um, my family moved here." I couldn't explain Dad's terrible life choices to them, and I was notoriously bad at making up lies on the spot. Liz was so much better at it than me. I couldn't lie my way off a burning airplane.

"Don't worry about it, Becks," Ashley said as she patted my arm in a gentle way. "She's just shy."

My toes curled inside my shoes at the sensation of her hand on my skin. God, I needed to get my attraction to her under control. I always did this when a pretty girl talked to me.

"Okay, so back to the lineup," Becky said, turning her attention away from me. "We need two more, and new girl here isn't on a team yet."

"Two more for what?" I said.

"The Academic Bowl," Ashley said. "It's the most competitive event of the year. Everyone wants to win. There are big prizes and it looks good on your college application. Becky and I want to form the best team possible."

"How are your grades?" Becky said. She leaned in, forcing her glasses to shift to perch on the end of her nose.

Oh god. I tried to swallow, but my throat was drier than a piece of sandpaper left in the middle of the desert. How were these girls already thinking about college when it was only our freshman year? My grades were okay. I had A's in Biology and Math, but a C in English. I just did not want to read books I did not want to read. Why high schools didn't assign students to read whatever we wanted in exchange for pizza like summer reading, I would never understand.

"If she's here, they're more than good," Ashley said. "You can't get in unless your grades are stellar, or unless your parents know somebody."

Know somebody. That's another piece of the puzzle that didn't add up. My grades weren't stellar, so it had to be that option, but who did Dad know that could get me into such an elite school last minute?

"Well, Jennifer?" Ashley said, prompting me when I didn't answer. "How are they?"

"My grades are pretty good," I said, suddenly finding my voice again. "I...can solve math equations like no one's business."

Ashley waved it off, as if that were all she needed to hear. "You're in! We meet after school on Tuesdays and Thursdays, and some on weekends when Becky isn't at ballet practice." She tapped her pencil to her glossy lips in thought. "Jennifer's got the math portions covered, but we still need one more. What about Marcus?"

Becky's whole body went stiff. Her voice got really quiet, real quick. "No way. I know you like him and all, but his family is into all that... *you* know."

Ashley rolled her eyes as hard as she could. "Don't be so judgy, Becks. He's a nice guy. And he won that award for writing last year, the one they said was impossible to get."

Becky's voice dropped even lower, so soft I had

to lean in to hear. "I don't think my mother's church group would feel comfortable having a *Blackwell* in our house."

"Maybe your Mom can just get over it," Ashley muttered as she scratched something out on her paper, as if she had just about had it with Becky's opinions.

"There are plenty of *other* people who can help us." Becky glanced back at Marcus over her shoulder. "Ones that don't have families into *that stuff.*"

Marcus Blackwell...just what is your family into? I snuck a peek over my shoulder. Marcus was staring directly at us, and his green eyes shone.

The door opened, revealing a guy with frizzy brown hair, round glasses, and who could have easily been John Mulaney's cousin. Stacks of notebooks teetered in his arms, and he was so tall he had to lean to get inside. He wasn't wearing the extremely tight jacket like everyone in this place. Instead, he rebelled by donning a simple white button-up shirt, rolled up to the elbows as if he were about to perform a dazzling magic trick. I'd known him all of five seconds and already had him pegged as the teacher mostly likely to have missed his calling as a stand-up comedian. Boy, did he pick the wrong school.

The Biology teacher heaved the notebooks on top of his desk. "I hope you all didn't stay up too late working on these presentations," the teacher said. "I know I did. I hate the number of tests they have us give you. Is everyone as beat as I am?"

His dad jokes were painted with a Southern accent much thicker than the rest. Southern accents were so diverse from state to state, but they could also vary in subregions of that particular state. His accent was pure Georgia, sure, but not the long drawl of Savannah or the lack of an obvious Southern accent from Atlanta. That placed him around the North Georgia mountains, possibly North Carolina.

He put his hand on his hip as he waited for laughs at his bad joke. When none came, he laughed. "I know, I know. The administration is trying to kill us, but at least we're in this together, right?" He scanned the room and his eyes landed on me. "Ah. You're new. I'm Mr. Castlebury, but you can call me Castlebury. The mister makes me feel like an old man. You just moved from Atlanta, is that right? Jennifer something."

"Yes, sir," I said. Everything in the south had to be punctuated with a "sir" or "ma'am" or you were completely disrespectful. "I'm Jennifer Strange."

He smiled approvingly. "What a cool name. Well, today should be fun. Presentations, no tests, or quizzes. That should give you a feel for how we do things around here." He clasped his hands together. "Now, who will be our first victim?" He scanned the room, eyes settling on a boy with dirty blonde hair and freckles who sat by the open windows. "Let's start with Brent, shall we?

I believe your research partner was Marcus?"

"Yes, absolutely." He fidgeted with a huge stack of papers as if being called on first was the worst thing to ever happen in his entire life. Looks like I wasn't the only one not fitting in with the Northwinds way of life.

"I got it." Marcus rushed over to help Brent gather their work. He whispered something to Brent and his shoulders relaxed at whatever Marcus said. They took the materials to the front of the room and did that awkward dance of who was going to read first in a content of politeness. Marcus shrugged and cleared his throat.

"Our research project is on the often-misplaced fear of sharks. We did extensive research on the history of shark attacks in the bay, and interviewed local sailors to get a better impression of what sharks are really like..."

I watched Marcus as he read, trying to get a better feel for him. I hadn't noticed before, but a silver chain glittered around his neck with a crystal the exact size, shape, and cut as mine, but it was so black it barely reflected the light. The horrible similarity made my palms itch.

"Ashley," I whispered. "What do you know about him?"

"Marcus?" she whispered back. "I've known him since elementary school. He moved here when we were seven. Something happened with his mom. He lives with his grandmother now."

"His grandmother?" I said.

She hesitated. "Yeah, she owns this antique shop."

"Girls. Seriously?" Castlebury shot us both a look.

"Sorry," Ashley said. "It won't happen again."

As Marcus read, I turned what she said over and over. What Ashley described wasn't so strange. I wished Castlebury hadn't cut her off. There was something about his family that was bad enough Becky wanted to avoid him. In the South, that usually meant one of two things: the Blackwell's were hiding something that didn't fit in with what was considered "proper," or they were into the occult.

I turned my attention back to the presentation. Marcus was droning on in the most boring way possible, but Brent wasn't looking at his paper or Castlebury or even the class—he was looking at me. He grinned, and his smile stretched so wide blood seeped out of the corners of his mouth. Red leaked between his teeth and smeared as it dripped down his chin.

"Oh my God," I said. I came to stand so fast my stool skidded on the linoleum. "He's bleeding!"

Marcus stopped reading. Ashley stared at me. Becky stared at me. *Everybody* stared at me.

Castlebury looked from me to Brent. "What blood? What did you see?"

"I'm sorry," I said. "Brent was just..."

The blood was gone. Brent was looking at me weird and they were all looking at me weird and

I just wanted to crawl under my desk and die. *Come on. Keep it together. It's not happening again. Breathe. Just breathe.*

"Sparrow." A horrible voice poured like thick slime into my ears. Hot breath sighed against my cheek. I whipped around; fist instinctively raised to punch whoever or whatever had just whispered to me. No one was there.

"Are you okay?" Ashley said. Her eyebrows knit together.

I turned to her, hating the concern that tinged her question. "I… I don't know."

"Jennifer, please." Castlebury pushed his glasses up his nose. "If you can't pay attention, I'm going to have to write you up. This is your last warning."

Acid churned and boiled in my stomach. The heat inside my body turned up all at once like I had been dropped in a steaming hot bath. Sweat trickled down my back and into the waistband of my skirt. *Oh no.* I knew this sick-to-my-stomach about-to-barf feeling. I'd had the same feeling yesterday at volleyball practice, but why was it back?

Don't throw up. For God's sake, not in front of everyone on your first day.

"You don't look so good," Ashley said.

I stumbled away from my stool, bent over, and vomited black sludge all over the linoleum.

Ashley got to her feet, stepping as far back from me as she could. "Oh my God."

"Eww," Becky said. "That's disgusting."

My lower lip trembled as I raised my hand. "Can I be excused?"

"Sure." Castlebury said. "It's down the hall to your—" He stopped mid-sentence.

"What is it?" I said.

"Your hair." Ashley covered her mouth with her hand.

My fingers shook as I reached up and touched something feathery floating around my head. My hair swam around my face like I was underwater, like I was freaking Ariel.

"What is happening to me?" I held up my hands. Blue ribbons like tiny cracks of lightning danced around my fingertips with a soft and violent light.

"It's okay." Castlebury's voice wavered. "It's just a static charge. We have to release it safely. There's a static bracelet in the cabinet that can help. Wait there. Don't panic."

Ashley reached out to touch my arm, but the static current snapped at her like a coiled snake. "Ow. What the heck? That really hurt. It isn't static. It's way worse."

"Get back," Caslebury said. "Don't touch her."

Black grew at the corners of my vision as the inside of my stomach boiled. The beaker in front of me vibrated and flung itself off the counter, shattering with a *pop*. Becky screeched and leapt away from the glass, but a large bit of shrapnel caught her in the leg. Blood snaked in a thin line down her calf and into her socks.

She fell to the floor, tears running her mascara

down both cheeks. "Oh my god, get it out!"

"Becky!" Ashley rushed to her side.

Her abandoned beaker slid off our granite countertop, plummeting to the floor with a *crack*. Another student's beaker went flying. And another. And another. The beakers kept coming, sliding off, one after the other, until the air filled with the *smash-crackle-pop* of broken glass. The other students fell into each other trying to escape, but they skidded on the shiny fragments littering the floor in every direction.

"Stay calm!" Castlebury yelled. "Follow me out into the hall!"

Everyone rushed for the classroom door at once, crowding the exit. A girl reached the door before him, attempted to move the handle, but from the click-click-click sound, it wasn't budging. The other students slid in the pooling water and fell into each other screaming. They clawed shoulders and ripped into arms to get out the door, but they jammed the exit like logs stopping a dam.

"It won't open!" the girl screamed.

"Move aside! I've got the key!" Castlebury had to elbow his way through the frantic students to reach the door.

The lock clicked and the door swung outward. Castlebury sent up a call for everyone to follow him. The second his foot planted outside the door slammed shut in his face. The howl of pain that followed was the worst sound I've ever heard in my entire life—complete and unbearable agony.

"Get his hand out!" Ashley cried.

The door opened and shut, opened, and shut. I wanted to run to Castlebury, wanted to help him, but my arms and legs wouldn't stop shaking. My body wouldn't cooperate, and I couldn't tell if it was because of the electricity waking up inside of me or the fear running like a jackrabbit through my veins. I caught a glimpse of Castlebury's broken hand between the sea of uniforms. Blood gushed down his knuckles and trailed from his wrist down to his elbow. There were holes where his index and middle fingers should have been.

A crackling sound rose and burst at the back of the room, like a soda bottle fizzing over. Liquid, green and frothing, sprayed from the beakers across the counter top onto an electrical outlet. Smoke billowed up to fill the ceiling, sending gray water pouring down from the sprinklers. In seconds, my uniform was soaked through to my skin. I rubbed my arms, a feeble attempt to slow my breathing, but each touch of my hands sent sparks flying off my skin. Was I the one causing this?

"Just stop!" I put my hands over my ears and screamed helplessly to no one, everyone, but mostly, myself. "Stop it!"

As the room swam with the percussive sounds of pain and fear, Marcus stood unmoving at the front of the room. The anger came off him in waves and sent an icy wind through my body. He was the only one who hadn't clambered for the exit, the only one who was not afraid. He knew what was happening and that it was because of *me.*

"Stop it!" Marcus yelled at me. "If you don't, you'll kill *everyone.*"

Lightning slithered around my body, itching to reach out to someone, something. That longing feeling in the pit of my stomach didn't want the students or Marcus.

"Sparrow."

That's not my name, but somehow, it's so achingly familiar.

I turned to follow the source of the voice that called for me, towards the thing at the back of the room. Brent stood in front of the cabinets filled with microscopes, but he no longer resembled the shy boy stumbling over his presentation. His eyes were black with thick rings of soot beneath them, his grin too wide, and he brought a hand to his mouth. Blood leaked in torrents out of his mouth, soaking the front of his shirt. He trailed one finger around his lips, painting the blood in a kind of smile.

"It's for you, Sparrow," he cooed, his voice dripping with adoration and love. **"I'm smiling for you."**

Water hammered against his face, but he didn't blink against the downpour. His face was so calm it was almost serene. Like he was happy. He lifted his hands, stretched them wide toward me with longing as he closed his eyes. **"Come** *to me, Sparrow."* Brent wanted me to hug him. He wanted to take me in his arms and squeeze me until I popped.

The thought that bubbled up inside of me was so horrible I didn't want to face it, didn't want to think. Dad had warned me about an entity far worse than what found me in the gym yesterday, and I guess it had finally found me. As the overhead lights flickered and burst in a shower of sparks, I had to accept the possibility.

Brent was possessed by a demon.

3

The Demon

THE LIGHTS WENT OUT all at once, as if someone had snuffed a candle out on the universe. I squinted into the dark, but nothing came in from the windows. *Impossible. Why was the sunlight gone?* There were half a dozen windows in the Biology classroom, but no light poured in from outside.

Something hit me in the face, thin and paper-cut sharp. I ran my hand across my cheek and my fingers bumped against something smooth. I took a sharp breath in and pulled until I held a bloody piece of something iridescent in my hand. Glass. It was a shard of broken glass.

I stumbled back until I collided with a desk. My chest heaved up and down so fast my ribcage ached. I took a deep breath, forcing my heart to slow. *Keep it together. Remember what Dad told you. Focus on actions, complete the next logical step. What did I need to do next? I need to see. I need light.* I pulled my cell phone out of my pocket and fumbled for the flashlight. I swiped it awake and turned the light away from me. The tiny, bright beacon glinted off a hundred pieces of broken glass swirling over the wet linoleum, flurrying around the room like a cloud of bats.

Someone took my arm and pulled me to them so violently, I skidded across a puddle.

"What the hell are you doing?" Marcus said. "Control your powers. You're going to get everyone here killed."

I ripped my arm from his grip. "*I'm* not doing this."

"Yes, you are." Something struck him in the back of the head. "What the—?"

"It's glass!" It was all I could manage to say before we were cut again.

"Sparrow," that horrible voice called. **"Can't you see me in the dark, Sparrow? I thought you birds could do anything."**

My cellphone shook in my hands as I whipped around to Brent—or rather, the bloody-mouthed person that used to be Brent. The bright camera light flickered when it found Bloody Mouth. It glistened off the dark trails on his neck and t-shirt.

"You know what I want," he said, spitting droplets of filthy water and blood at me. **"Release**

me from this flesh prison."

"I don't know what you're talking about!" I screamed.

He floated across the room, toes dragging little currents through the water, and grabbed a student by the base of his neck.

"Release me, Sparrow," he said as the poor student squirmed. **"Give me a body of my own."**

"I can't!" I said.

Bloody Mouth's face cooled. He studied me with wet, pleading eyes, and then brought his victim's face crashing down into the black hardtop of my desk. Bloody Mouth smashed, and smashed, and smashed until the student's face turned to putty. My cellphone turned hot in my hands so fast, I dropped it into the water. It sizzled as it sank into a puddle. "Great! There goes my light."

"Jennifer! Come on!" Marcus pleaded, snapping my attention back to Bloody Mouth. "Just kill it already!"

"I'm trying!" My hands itched and pulsed with a pressure so powerful, they shook like a fire hydrant about to burst. *Don't use your gift,* Dad said. *Not for any reason, no matter how much it hurts. Hold back, or you will kill everyone.* Marcus wanted me to kill whatever was inside Bloody Mouth, just like my body. I clenched my fists, suppressing the urge as much as I could. No one was going to die because of me.

Bloody Mouth turned to Ashley. She clutched

a frightened Becky as hard as she could, tears streaming as she glared at his lolling tongue and blackened mouth. He grabbed Ashley by the throat and squeezed. She clawed at him, trying to breathe, her face contorted with pain. Blue lightning erupted from my palms and hit Bloody Mouth in his back. He released her and whirled around, sweeping the electricity away to strike the fluorescent lights along the ceiling. The bulbs whizzed until they burst in a shower of sparks. Dad never said anything about my powers and the freaking light show. If I get out of this alive, we are going to have a long, horrible chat.

"Jennifer!" Marcus said. "Aim for his head!"

"Stop telling me what to do!" I whipped around to send another round of lightning at Bloody Mouth, but he dove behind Castlebury's desk.

"Seriously, Sparrow?" Marcus yelled. "How did you miss him? He was right there!"

"Stop bullying me!" I yelled.

"Fine." Marcus pulled something out of his pocket. "I'll deal with it."

"I'll show you dealing with it!" My hands flushed with heat as I thrust both palms at the desk. Bloody Mouth laughed as he faded away from me, vanishing into the dark corner of the room. Smoke rolled all around him, filling the room until I couldn't see. I ran into the grey.

"Where are you?" I yelled and sucked in a mouthful of dust. I coughed hard as a sharp object punched me square in the waist. It was hard and smooth with something squishy that crumbled in my hands when I touched it. Soggy papers. Folders. It was Castlebury's desk.

"Sparrow." The hair at the back of my head rustled. **"I'm right here."**

He yanked my hair into a ball and pulled. I screeched as he tossed me across the floor and my ribs slammed against a desk. I lay still, struggling to breathe in as dirty water pooled between my teeth every time I opened my mouth. Dad's voice cut through the ringing in my ears, calm and steady: *If one of them attacks you, use your mother's necklace, use the sigils—do anything to keep the entity from touching you.*

I grabbed the rose quartz and held it out towards him like a shield, but the blue current leapt from my hands and snapped at the chain. Bloody Mouth laughed as the crystal slipped right off my neck and fell into the water with a plop. I rolled over and felt my way around as careful as I could, but it was no use. My one protection was lost among the glass shards and gray water.

No. Not lost.

The journal.

Where is the journal?

The classroom door swung open with a bang.

"What in the Sam Hill is going on in here?" a woman bellowed. The teacher from the front office, the one who looked at me like I was a bug, stood in the doorway—Miss something or other. Hallway light spilled inside, illuminating everything I both did and did not want to see. Students lay everywhere, broken and bleeding. The desks lay discarded, overturned on their sides, and splintered. All of the glass shelves inside the cabinets were gone, littering the floor in diamond pieces.

"Everyone out right now!" the administrator yelled, but her voice broke apart as the smoke cleared and revealed the wreckage of the classroom, the students, and our teacher.

"Come on!" Ashley said, searching the faces of everyone and no one. Despite the pieces of glass jutting out of her shoulder, she lifted Becky over her shoulder, but her body was also a porcupine of shards. A girl and boy stumbled out, but the glass in their arms and legs made it difficult to walk they limped out the door. Castlebury lay unmoving, curled up around his hand—passed out from blood loss or dead, I couldn't tell. No one else got up. They were all who survived. I dug my fingernails into my arms until my skin hurt. It's my fault, all of it. *My fault.*

Ashley rushed into the room, water kicking up around her as she ran.

"You can't go back in there!" the administrator said, pleading for her to come back.

"There are still some people left!" Ashley said. "Jennifer, Marcus—Come on!"

She turned around and reached a gentle hand for me. Red trailed down from the glass in her shoulder to her elbow.

"I'm sorry," I said. "I didn't mean for any of this to happen."

"Jennifer, it's okay," she said, eyes wincing with pain. "Take my hand."

I let go of my arms. Something struck her in the back of the head and Ashley crumpled to the floor like a discarded doll.

"Ashley!" Marcus yelled, but I couldn't see him.

Bloody Mouth stood behind her. His right hand dripped with thick blood.

I rushed to her side and flipped her over to get her face out of the puddle.

"What are you doing, Brent?" The administrator took a step towards us, but the door slammed in her face. The lock gave a decided click, shutting her up. She jiggled the handle, pounded on the door, but it wouldn't budge. Everything was dark again, save for that little bit of light coming in from the tiny window over the door. It was just Marcus, Ashley, and me, but I had no idea where either Bloody Mouth or Marcus went. The smoke was still so thick.

I kneeled beside Ashley and shook her, hard. "Come on. You can do it. Come back to me." Her eyes did not open. I tried to breathe, but my ribs felt too tight. *This is my fault—the demon, the debris, the chaos—my fault. They found me, just like the ghost in Atlanta, only this time Dad wouldn't be here to get rid of it. I have to protect her. I'm not going to let one more person die because of me.*

Sneakers squeaked across the floor behind me. "Sparrow!" Marcus yelled. "Get out of the way!"

Something white and small was in his right hand. It was the color of bleached coral, but it was crescent in shape. *A knife?*

Marcus yelled as he leapt at his possessed friend. Bloody Mouth backhanded him, sending Marcus's body flying as if he weighed no more than a fly. Marcus hit one of the cabinets at the back of the room with a shuttering clang and slid to the floor. I waited for a few breathless moments for him to pick himself back up, go in swinging.

"Sparrow," Bloody Mouth said. *"You're not watching."*

Something slammed into my side so hard my body went tumbling into an upturned desk, hitting the same bruise in my ribs from the time he tossed me earlier. *Get up, Jacks. Marcus isn't coming. He isn't going to save you. Dad isn't going to save you. Do something!* I scrambled to get up to my knees and Bloody Mouth leapt on top of me before I could roll over.

"At last." The heat of Bloody Mouth's rotten breath wet my cheek. He pressed down on my chest so hard my ribcage smushed against my lungs. *"Release me."*

"I'm not giving you what you want." A crackling sound emanated from my fingertips. Blue lightning sparked from my palms and illuminated Bloody Mouth's delighted eyes. "I won't release you."

A piece of his flaking cheek skin loosened and fell into my mouth. He tasted like pennies and ash and—*oh God*. I spit it out and clawed at his shirt, trying to push him off without touching his skin, but he pressed down more. Black filled my vision as my brain sped like a freight train down a tunnel towards passing out. The pressure in my hands became too unbearable.

"Don't touch someone possessed," he said, like it was all so easy. *"Run away."*

So much for that, Dad.

"Release me NOW, SPA—"

He released me. The sudden air in my lungs surprised me and I choked. The coughing fit that followed was so deep and painful, the floor swam beneath me in waves. Marcus's hard eyes were so blurry I had trouble focusing on his face as I tried to find my breath again, but it wasn't coming. He held the white knife against Bloody Mouth's throat and his skin sizzled where the blade met his jaw. I rolled away from them to kneel. It was hard to tell where one of them ended and another person began, and my stomach cramped from the lack of oxygen. My legs wobbled as a splash came up around my shoes. There was a face between my sneakers—Marcus's face.

"Fight," he said, and closed his eyes.

Don't fight. *Don't fight.*

No, Dad. I'm sorry. I can't keep my promise.

Bloody Mouth rushed at me and I didn't think. I arched my fist back and punched, releasing

all the power bottled up inside of me. Blue light
exploded the room as Bloody Mouth's skin smoked
in the cup-shaped print where my hand landed.

"Yes. Yes. YES!" Bloody Mouth stumbled away
from me. He screamed and laughed and clawed
at what remained of his face. There was a great
POP! A gust of wind hit me square in the stomach
along with a wet splattering sound that went out
in all directions.

What...just happened?

Sunlight spilled in from the windows, leaving
what was left of the classroom on full display. All
of the desks were thrown, tossed, or completely
exploded apart. The stools lay on their sides or
upturned and there was glass all over the damn
place. Filthy gray water soaked the classroom,
immersing the linoleum by a couple inches. I
vaguely made out the distant sounds of students
clamoring and crying on the other side of the
door, and the voice of a teacher telling them to
get back, to not look at what was inside the room.

I raised a hand to my cheek, finding a bit of
wet, solid debris there. I wiped the gunk off of my
face enough to see. Marcus stood panting a few
feet away, covered in something red and white
and yellow. Ashley lay a few feet away, her chest
rising and falling as if in sleep.

My hands. There was more gunk all over my
hands. Red Jell-O squished between my fingers.
Bits and pieces of something white and hard and
red trailed across the floor in all directions, like

red chili had leaked through the ceiling. *Where is Bloody Mouth?*

I picked up something more solid and pink. A fingernail, a knuckle, freckles. It was a human finger. And then it hit me where Bloody Mouth had gone.

My stomach boiled up my throat as I leaned on a nearby desk and tried not to vomit.

"Sparrow?" Someone touched my shoulder. I clutched my heart as I turned to find Marcus. Cuts ran up his neck, across his cheeks, and along the backs of his hands. He had changed clothes sometime during the fight. He wore a jean jacket covered in black and white embroidered patches with all sorts of signs and symbols I didn't recognize.

"What do you want?"

He reached for my face. "Let me look at you."

I shook my head. Everything between my ears felt about ten times too big.

Marcus grabbed my chin and forced me to look at him. "Sorry. I need to know for sure."

My stomach rolled. "Let me go!"

His face was so close to mine, but I couldn't bring myself to look in his eyes. They would actually be nice to look at if he weren't being so strange and horrible and vague. I'd never known despair like this, so deep and complete. *Brent. This is my fault. No. Not mine. Dad's* fault.

"Please, look at me," he said, and it was a gentle request this time. "I need to know for sure."

I did it. I looked at him, but I poured all the venom in my veins and the ice in my heart into the glare I shot back at him. I had no desire to know him, no need to learn anything more about this jerk who had yelled at me when all I needed was guidance.

Marcus's eyes widened. "You are the Sparrow, but not the competent one, not the one who banishes instead of summoning."

"I think you are... the worst person... I've ever met." I leaned over and vomited on his shoes.

"That's just...great," he said.

"Sorry." I wiped my mouth. "I just couldn't stand looking at your face anymore."

I turned away in case he didn't get the hint I was going to ignore whatever he said back at me. Only an hour ago, this was a normal classroom with posters and presentations and beakers. Now, I was walking through a hell scene straight out of a Bosch painting. Blood pooled in little rivers between the upturned desks and splattered across the white board in wide arcs. The guy on the floor with the piece of glass in his eye was definitely dead. Castlebury still lay behind his desk, clutching his bloody stump of a broken hand, but he moaned in his sleep. I hadn't killed my teacher. I closed my eyes, unable to look at it anymore. This had to be a dream. Nothing in real life could ever be this horrible. I wanted to wake up. *Just let me wake up*.

Mom's necklace didn't work. It was supposed to

be safe now. The crystal was supposed to protect me. That's what Dad had said. That's what he promised, but he was so unbelievably wrong. It hadn't protected me or anyone else at all.

I opened my eyes and lifted my foot out of the water. My socks were soaked through from the water and blood. The white cotton had turned a nasty shade of mud brown.

"Jennifer! I said move!" he yelled.

Marcus leaned back into my field of view. He gripped his knife tight in his hand as he came to his feet. He braced himself as if he were about to lunge at something behind me.

"What are you—" I said but I never finished the thought.

A great black tongue licked slowly up the side of my face. A voice like a whisper of a rattlesnake tickled the inside of my ear.

"Sparrow. You taste delicious."

The monster that licked me was bigger than I could have possibly imagined. It filled the classroom with its accordion-like body. Shiny ink dripped down impossibly long arms that bent forward like an orangutan. Round, pearl eyes rested in the center of its snake-like head where six flaring nostrils split its face above its wide slit of a mouth. The rest of its body was a long mass—gray and muscular, with a coiled tail that dragged behind it. It was too horrible to take in. My mind leapt from feature to feature without settling too long in one area or I would start screaming.

But the voice—that was the worst part of all.
It was the voice of Bloody Mouth.

4

The Gift

AFTER THE GHOST ATTACKED me during volleyball practice, Dad told me he knew what was coming to find me next. He said that while the ghost we just faced was terrible, and more would come looking for me, demons were much, much worse. Ghosts were once human, he said, but now they're stuck between the living and the dead, doomed to repeat their mistakes. At their heart, they are still human. I'd listened to him and accepted this, but his next instruction made absolutely no sense until this moment.

"Demons, however, are a completely different beast. They have no bodies of their own and must possess a host in order to survive. Unless they swallow every bite of their host's soul, possession is

temporary. Never touch them. Never. Promise me."

As I took in the full behemoth of the demon that was Bloody Mouth, the fragments of Dad's words fell neatly into place. The horrible truth of the Sparrow power bloomed fully in my mind. I knew why that ghost wanted me in the gym back home, and why this demon possessed a host to force me to touch its skin. I understood why Dad said to never lay a hand on someone who was possessed.

That's the Sparrow power. I can give ghosts and demons a body.

"Unexpected, this body." The creature rolled its shoulders, assessed the supple nature of its limbs. The creature swung its massive head towards the lifeless body of the boy with the glass in his eye. **"Unexpected, this hunger."**

Bloody Mouth slithered over to the body and unhinged his jaw like a great python, He struck the upper torso with his needle teeth.

Marcus. Ashley. Castlebury. Brent.

This is my fault. If I hadn't touched Brent, he would still be alive. The demon Bloody Mouth sucked the dead guy further inside, eating and licking him like he was some kind of meat popsicle. A few more swallows and he would be completely gone. No. He tricked me. He forced me into choosing myself or Brent. Blue lightning danced around my fists.

"Hey! Bloody Mouth!"

As he turned his big head, the white blade

whistled through the air. Marcus had used the distraction to make a leap for Bloody Mouth. The demon whipped one of its long arms around and slammed him in the stomach. I screamed as he went flying into the whiteboard with a smack. One of the stools toppled with a clang as Marcus connected with it on his descent to the floor. He crumbled like a discarded piece of paper. My fire roared around my arms. No. I can't use my power again. I don't know what it will do. The banishment sigils. *Where the hell is my bag?* I scrambled across the room searching for it in the filthy water.

Bloody Mouth swallowed the last of the dead boy and cackled at Marcus. ***"Come on, boy. I've survived the ages, and I will survive you."***

Marcus kicked the stool away. He straightened by the whiteboard, wiped a bunch of blood from his mouth, and staggered into the wall. He was going to get himself killed. If he got knocked across the room like that one more time, that was it.

I sloshed and grasped around the filthy water until my hands met a familiar strap. The upturned desk had pinned my book bag and I had to yank hard to release it. *Oh no.* My heart pounded as I removed Dad's journal from the sloppy canvas mess that used to be my book bag. I turned it over, inspecting all sides as quick as I could as Bloody Mouth's back bristled, preparing to launch at Marcus. Water stained the edges of the pages, but the thick leather kept most of the damage out. It was okay, would be okay. I just needed the banishment ward. Crap. Where was it? This sort of information should have been on page one.

Bloody Mouth leapt and Marcus's knife whistled through the air as he lunged to meet the wide, hungry mouth. The blade landed in its thick neck with a squirting sound as the demon's jaw clamped around Marcus's shoulder. Spouts of inky blood poured from the wound, spraying Marcus in the face. A rotten egg smell flooded everything with a stench so rotten I heaved, but there was nothing left in my stomach. The demon writhed around the room, knocking over desks and chairs, disappearing into a cloud of its hissing flesh. The dust cloud billowed so high everything went dark again.

I flipped to the correct page and pressed my finger against the Banishment sigil. *"You can draw it on paper or cloth."* I didn't have paper, but the journal—it was technically paper. Would it work if I just shoved the book at the demon?

Bloody Mouth wheezed as he released Marcus from his jaws and rolled his big head to look at me. ***"You keep that away."***

I returned its shark-mouth grin with a shrug. "Oh, you're afraid of this?"

I opened the journal and shoved the Banishment sigil at the demon. Its pasty gray skin turned hot; its inky flesh erupted into brilliant flame. It shrieked and released Marcus, stumbled backwards over desks and stools. Marcus winced as he held onto the demon's neck, keeping it close to the book while it burned.

"You weren't supposed to kill me!" it howled.

The demon cried in terrible agony and writhed like snake with its head cut off, but it couldn't escape the blaze erupting across its body. His gray lips curled back, parting the fog with a smile revealing rows of those needle-like teeth. He laughed long and hard as his body withered away, smothered like ash rising from a doused campfire. Bloody Mouth glowered at Marcus with a hatred so fierce I thought he might catch on fire too.

"She will have your head for this," Bloody Mouth said.

In a rush of wind, the demon was gone.

Marcus struggled, clutching his shoulder to stop the blood. "I hate Wraiths," he said. "They're such a freaking pain. Won't get the stink out of this jacket for days. Nice going, Sparrow, letting one loose."

"A Wraith?" I said, closing the book and hugging it my chest. I thought I saw an entry about a Wraith when I had flipped through the journal last night, but I didn't get a good look.

He gaped at me like I could not have possibly said anything dumber. "You mean you don't even know what a Wraith is?" He rolled his eyes. "Why am I not surprised?"

"How was I supposed to know?" I said.

He actually face-palmed. "How would you not

know your demons? You're the *Sparrow*."

Blue lightning winked across my fingers as my face flushed. "Why does everyone keep calling me the Sparrow?"

Marcus straight up ignored me. He walked over to his book bag and retrieved it from a puddle in the back of the room. He shook it off and cleaned it as if it were more important than anything I had to say. God, what a jerk.

I sighed, clutching my journal like a life preserver. "So, I messed up. Okay. But this isn't my fault. I don't know what's happening to me."

"I can't believe the Sparrow doesn't know what a Wraith is," Marcus muttered as he inspected the wound. "Might as well say a spider doesn't know what a web is."

"There's a much bigger elephant in this room," I said. "You know what a Wraith is, who the Sparrows are, and you even have some sort of knife to fight them. Who are you? Why is everyone afraid of you?"

"Everyone knows the Sparrows," he said. His hands trembled as he cleaned his blade with a rag he'd retrieved from his bag. As he worked, I got a better look at his jacket. The patches weren't like one of those singers on the cover of Dad's old 80s vinyl—They were drawings. No, they were wards in black and white, and they looked exactly like the drawings from Dad's journal. The similarities between us were stacking, but Marcus wasn't just into the occult or a Wiccan or something like I thought earlier. He was a part of that world—Dad's ghost hunting world.

"My dad told me no one else knew about the Sparrows," I said, but he went on ignoring me. I clenched my fist. "I know I messed up. There's nothing I can do to bring them back, but you know about all this. Help me. Please"

He sighed. "Sorry. I tend to get...shaken after these things. Believe it or not, I hate fighting demons. I can't stand what it takes to send them packing, or the carnage they leave, but no. I can't help you. There's no way to stop your power. You have to learn to control it, and only an experienced medium can teach you that, or another Sparrow."

Mom. She could have taught me, but she was gone. I pressed the journal against my chest, but the pressure did nothing to slow my breathing. Dad wanted to get something to help me, something more powerful than the rose quartz. Then it hit me, something the demon had said. "Why did the Wraith say you weren't supposed to kill it? Who is going to have your head for this?"

That got his attention. His expression melted into a blank calm. "I don't know what the Wraith meant. He probably just didn't want to be killed."

My stomach turned cold. He was lying. I gritted my teeth as I tried to calm myself down. "Did someone send the Wraith?"

He said nothing.

"You know about all this," I said, my voice rising.

"Did someone send the demon that possessed Brent? How did the Wraith find me?"

He pocketed the knife. "You're the Sparrow of Summoning." He gestured to the room around him. "And this is the result of a Summoner who doesn't know how to control her power. The demon comes, takes a host, uses the Sparrow to release itself from the host, and a whole mess ensues. You're a beacon every ghost can see for a hundred miles around. You think a demon wouldn't notice you?"

He was changing the subject. He knew I'd caught him, but I didn't know if he was lying or telling the truth about Sparrows being a beacon. "You tell me."

"No." He folded his arms, revealing more of the nasty gash in his bicep. "You brought this whole situation on yourself by coming to one of the most haunted cities in America. Savannah is a hotbed for ghosts and demons, and you chose to live here. Are you really that naïve?"

I tucked my chin until my hair covered my face. "I don't know why I'm here, okay? A ghost attacked me at my school yesterday, and my dad's response was to drop me in Savannah last night. He left me with my sister and gave me this stupid journal and said 'I have to go. Bye. Figure it out!' He didn't tell me anything about myself or my powers or my past. I was just expected to figure it out for myself."

He paused. "He left you here last night?"

My chest tightened as he walked over to me.

"Jennifer," he said. Horror tinged his voice as he covered his mouth. "Your arms."

"What are you talking about?" I glanced down, more out of annoyance than actual curiosity, and gasped. Gold flakes painted the backs of my hands, marked my skin from my fingertips to my forearms. They covered my freckles, all the little hairs, *everything*, as if I'd dipped my arms into a paint bucket. I raked my nails against my skin, but the marks didn't budge. They glittered in defiance and had no intention of going anywhere.

I almost dropped the journal as I stumbled back. "What the hell is happening to me?"

"Equivalent exchange," he said. "You brought something over, something has to go back. You're being pulled over into the Other."

He met my eyes, full of pity, and that burned me more than anything else he'd done or said since I met him. I didn't want his pity. I didn't want his stupid face looking at me with sadness. I opened my mouth to demand an explanation, but the classroom door burst open. Several people dressed all in yellow tumbled inside. Firefighters. The administrator must have called the fire department, the police, *everybody*.

"Oh, holy Jesus," the lead firefighter said. "What the hell happened in here?"

"Are you all right, ma'am?" said another firefighter, her voice muffled by a plastic mask.

She came to me and assessed the damage. She

checked my cuts and bruises and asked me to breathe as deeply as I could into the mask she shoved over my face. I coughed hard and it took a few moments before I could stop. A team of people leaned down to check Castlebury and called on the walkie for a stretcher.

"We need to get this one to the ambulance," she told the other firefighters as she nodded at me. "There might be some lung damage."

She put an air mask over my face and wrapped me in blankets. Clean air, sweet and pure, entered my lungs from the mask. As I breathed, my vision blurred and my head swam, but I could make out Marcus. He was being led away by a firefighter who fussed over his wounds, but he remained as stoic as ever. Marcus turned back to me, a quick glance, but his eyes were wide and watery. More stupid pity.

"I don't feel so good," I told the firefighter leading me out of the room. The floor came up fast. After that, all I saw was black.

I wish I was out hunting rather than being sent away to Savannah for a year of study. This year will be my first on my own. I'm eighteen. I should be out in the field or going to college, but no. It's not "what's always been done." My family are known to be seekers of knowledge more than they are to be killers of the paranormal and impossible. If we had a crest, I'm sure it would be of a knight slaying a dragon, not some scholar trapped in his tower of study. I don't know why Dad is making me do this. I'd rather be out there fighting. My brothers tell me it's a privilege to study under another family, especially one as prestigious as Arturo's family. Dad isn't giving me some gift. What he's giving me is a death sentence. I'd rather be doing anything other than cooped up in some library studying under some old guy. Although, my older brother Jet tells me that Arturo has two girls in his care that are the most powerful links to the other side that have ever existed.

That might be a sight worth seeing.

Jacob
January 31, 1991

5

Liz

SOMETHING PULSED NEAR MY head, a steady mechanical heart beat. I'd heard this sound only in movies before, but it was clearly a monitor. Someone wheezed in and out, rasping through a snorkeling mask. My chest rose and fell with the rhythm of the sound. It was me, my breath. My eyes blinked into the bright, florescent lights of a hospital room. Teal curtains blocked the doorway to the outside hall and there was a painting of little sailboats on a vast, blue ocean on the wall in front of me. I lay in a little bed with cold bars close to a monitoring station. Tubes ran from a clear bag into my right arm. Something covered my mouth, constricting my face. I touched the smooth plastic of the oxygen mask. I didn't want anything there. Nothing on my face! I yanked it off.

"Stop," Liz said. "You need to breathe."

My sister sat in a chair next to me. Her thick, blonde mane tumbled down her shoulders in a tangle of knots. No matter what she did, her hair was always falling and half-falling out of her top-knot bun. Dots of white and pink paint freckled the fabric of her overalls and striped tank top. Mascara formed little half-moon rings under her eyes. She'd been crying, hard from the look of her blotchy cheeks. I'd never seen her this worried. Guess all that irritation with me was completely gone now, but I didn't want to gloat. I hadn't meant to make her worry.

Behind her, a nurse in blue scrubs came and checked my IV bag. She tapped the liquid and it sloshed around a little. "You're almost done with this one. I'll let the doctor know you're awake."

As soon as the nurse closed the door, Liz teared up again. "I'm so glad you're okay. I'm sorry I was such a jerk to you this morning."

She took my hand, squeezed, and I squeezed back. My hand glittered in hers. I gasped and yanked away from Liz. *The mark. It's still there. Damn. Guess it wasn't a bad dream after all.*

"What are you doing?" Liz said, clearly hurt I had pulled away from her.

There was no use hiding anymore. I held up my hands. "I should explain how I got this gold mark..."

57

She shrugged. "What mark?"

My whole body numbed. Liz couldn't see it. I really was the only one with powers. Dad was right; Liz didn't know about any of this, hadn't manifested any Sparrow abilities as a teen. Her inability to see the mark explained why the nurse hadn't mentioned it either. My body unclenched a little. In a way, the mark being invisible to most people was a relief. If the nurse could see it, I would probably be kept under lock and key. I'd be studied by doctors and trapped here until another demon found me.

Dad told me not to tell Liz, but if Marcus was right and I was a beacon for the supernatural in a city filled with ghosts, more would be on the way. I hadn't even lasted one day. How long could I realistically go without telling her?

"I want to talk, but not here." My mask wheezed as I turned to look out the dark window at the moon peaking between the curtains. "How long was I out?"

"A few hours." She still sounded hurt.

"The last thing I remember is this woman in yellow—a firefighter. She must have brought me to the hospital. Oh no. The journal." I pushed myself up to sit and ripped the mask off. "I can't think with this on."

"What are you doing?" she said. "You need to rest."

"If I keep this on for one more second, I'm going to have a full-blown panic attack."

She tried to get me to keep the mask on, but I smacked her hand away. Once removed, it revealed something else stuck to my face. I ran my fingers across the rough bandage taped over my cheek, in the space where the glass struck me. It must have cut my face more than I thought. I pulled the sheets back, revealing my legs. There weren't any cuts, just some bruises, but both of my knees were raw.

I searched the bedsheets, the floor, and the little table on my bedside. No journal. It was gone. I had no way to defend myself. I clenched the sheets until my knuckles turned white. A tear dropped on the flowers of my paper-thin hospital gown.

"I'm such an idiot," I said. "How could I lose it?"

"Whoa," Liz said. "What are you talking about?"

"Dad's journal. It's gone."

Her brow furrowed. "No, they found something like that. It came in with you. They said they had a tough time prying it out of your hands."

I wiped my nose. "Did they find a leather book the size of a very small dog?"

She shrugged. "Yes. It's pretty gross though. Are you sure you still want it?" She handed the journal to me and I snatched it from her.

She raised her hands, backing away. "Whoa. Glad I didn't toss it in the trash can."

I clutched the water-stained journal to my chest and didn't care how it made me cry. It was safe. Dad's journal and all of the answers were safe. I'd never let it out of my sight again. It had saved us from the Wraith. *Marcus. Ashley. What happened to them?* I needed to ask Marcus about equivalent exchange. Maybe the firefighters brought him to the hospital too.

"What happened to the other students?" I asked.

Liz shrugged. "I don't know. I got the call from your school there was a fire and that you were in the hospital. Don't worry about that right now. The important thing is that you're okay. We'll do everything we can to help you get better."

That's something I'd heard Mom say, but now it was coming out of Liz's mouth. The displaced words rubbed me all wrong, like I'd accidentally swallowed a spider. Just because Mom was gone didn't mean Liz needed to sound like her. I wanted to roll my eyes at her, but I needed her on my side. I swallowed my venom and sighed.

"I wanted to see if my friends were okay," I said, and that was true. "Some of them got really hurt."

Liz sighed. "I wish I knew more, but I don't. I hope your friends are okay too. I didn't realize you'd made friends so fast."

The door opened. A doctor with long, black hair tied behind her neck in a low ponytail entered the room cradling a manila folder in her arms. From her hair and the way her smile stretched into her eyes and made them twinkle, she reminded me so much of Ashley.

"Hello, Jennifer. I'm Doctor Gerard," she said. Her voice was so calm and smooth, like she came in to read me a bedtime story. "We've been monitoring you for a few hours, and things look good. You didn't receive any lung damage. I think it's safe for you to go home, provided you rest. The cough might linger for a few days."

Dr. Gerard turned to address Liz. "I'm writing a prescription for an inhaler. Make sure she uses it every four to six hours." She scribbled something on a clipboard. "You'll need to fill out these forms to release her. You *are* her legal guardian, right?"

"Yes," Liz said, but she didn't sound as confident as she thought she did.

"Is Ashley okay?" I blurted out. "Is everyone else okay?"

Dr. Gerard stopped writing. "Ashley? Ashley Gerard? She's my daughter."

I clutched the journal to suppress the hot guilt worming around in my stomach. "She was with me when it happened."

She gave me a tired smile. "She's recovering well. You girls were lucky. That school should have evaluated the old wires that run through the building better. If they had, that fire wouldn't have happened in the first place."

Electrical fire? So that's how they're covering everything up.

"I'm glad both of you are okay," Dr. Gerard continued. "Ashley is fine, and so are the other students. Go home with your sister. Rest." She handed Liz the papers and prescription sheet. "Take these to the front when you check out."

She removed my IV tube. "Please give me a call if you have any questions on the dosage. My number is on the top of the sheet."

Liz held the paperwork to her chest like she'd just been given the most sacred of documents. "Absolutely. You can count on me."

Doctor Gerard smiled a very knowing smile at both of us, as if she had figured out Liz wasn't exactly my legal guardian, but she wasn't going to say anything. Before she left the room, she added, "I'll have Ashley contact you when she's feeling up to it."

"Thank you. And Doctor Gerard?" I said. "Is there a Marcus Blackwell here?"

She paused. "Normally, I'm not allowed to give out patient information. But I can tell you the name Marcus doesn't ring a bell. If he's not here, take comfort that he is probably fine."

She shut the door.

Damn. He's not here, and neither is my phone. The internet. I'd check online when I got home to my computer.

I looked down and remembered my hospital gown. I'm not surprised they'd stripped me clean, put my disgusting uniform in a bag, and wiped me down with sponges. My uniform was probably covered in Wraith guts, blood, and dirty ceiling water. Still, I couldn't leave the hospital with my butt hanging out.

"Please tell me you brought me something else to wear," I said.

Liz scooped up a duffle bag and unzipped it to reveal a pair of jeans and a t-shirt. She tossed them over to me. "Got you covered. I have a couple other options. Even some underwear. I wasn't sure how long we would be here, so I brought a few pairs."

The shirt was from my first concert, a three-day festival with all my favorite singers called Lilith Fair. Mom took me when I was young, one of the few times she ever left the house. I wore that shirt even though it was still way too big for me. I still liked to wear it when I was sick or exhausted or lonely, and Liz had been paying attention.

"How did you know?" I said.

"Know what?" she said.

"That I would want to wear this shirt."

She smiled at me. "What are sisters for?"

"How are you always this prepared?" I rolled my eyes at her, but really, my heart warmed. When I needed it most, she was always there for me.

She grabbed my bag of old clothes and got a full whiff of rotten egg from the Wraith. "Ugh. Why does this smell like rotten bananas and ass?"

I laughed. "You don't want to know."

Amelia

Emily

Staying with Arturo was a huge mistake. He wakes me before the sun's up, insists I scrub the floorboards of his "scrying parlor" (whatever that means), makes me clean his boots, dust his old books, and every other menial task he can think of. I thought I was supposed to be learning about ghosts, not playing housemaid to the world's jerkiest jerk. The only part of my lessons where I actually learned anything new was symbology. I took a few notes on some of the more interesting and useful sigils.

The only good part of my day is when I catch a glimpse of Emily Sparrow. She is the most beautiful girl I've ever seen. I only get to see her when I clean the scrying parlor. She and her sister Amelia are always there meditating. Arturo keeps telling them to focus and concentrate on bringing their Sparrow powers together, but I don't know what that means. Arturo won't tell me, and his wife is always out collecting more haunted antiques for their "side business."

Emily has the prettiest red hair I've ever seen. Her sister Amelia doesn't like me at all. She keeps giving me this nasty look whenever I'm in there cleaning. Maybe I can convince her to let me see Emily if I give her one of those cakes. I know where Arturo keeps them locked away in the back cabinet. I'll try that and see what happens.

Jacob
Feb 12, 1991

6

City of the Dead

RAIN PATTERED AGAINST THE hood of the car as Liz parked in front of her apartment and cut the engine. The little white bag from CVS sat in my lap on top of Dad's journal. It was filled with pills and an inhaler, along with several empty Doritos bags, and Coke cans. We had devoured the snacks the second we'd bought them. My vision drifted in static waves. Every inch of my body ached like it had been put through a mulcher. All I wanted was sleep, but my hair stuck together in clumps and smelled like a filthy river had a dinner date with the blood of a thousand dead rats.

"Are you okay?" Liz leaned back in the driver's seat to look at me.

"I hate that question." I turned away from her to stare out into the rain, but I couldn't see much of the surrounding trees and brick buildings. The rain was so heavy in Savannah when it fell you could hardly see anything at all.

Liz pushed a stray wet hair out of her eyes. "Sorry. You were gone for a second."

I sighed. "I know. I didn't mean to snap. I just don't want to talk about it."

"About what happened at school?" she said.

I wished she wouldn't pressure me. I guess I understood. I did tell her we had to talk, several times, but reliving what happened today was the absolute last thing I wanted to do. The images played over and over in my mind, the same way a horror movie stuck in my head long after I watched it. I closed my eyes and saw Ashley fall slowly into dark water, Marcus gut the Wraith with his knife, and Brent paint blood around his mouth. I saw the electricity that whispered across my fingertips whenever I called. My body was too exhausted to go through the emotional steps of reliving the play-by-play. I didn't need a talk; I needed a nap.

"I don't know if I feel safe," I muttered to the empty parking lot.

"What do you mean?" Liz asked.

Great. She's worried now. Just stop talking.

I sighed. "Nothing. I don't know what I'm saying. I'm tired. It's been *a day*."

She put her hand on my arm. "I know we haven't talked in months, but I'm here. If there's something you want to get off your chest. You can talk to me."

I rolled my eyes. She couldn't claim she would be there for me after so many months of not talking. "It was more like a year," I said. "We honestly haven't talked since you left for SCAD."

She bit her lip for a moment and thought about her wording before she continued. "I understand. I'll be here. You know...when you're ready."

She opened the door and stepped out into the rain, leaving me alone in the front seat. Liz hadn't offered to talk to me in... Okay, I couldn't remember the last time we had talked about anything. Even though I hated the way she treated me, I was grateful she acknowledged our broken relationship, but it wasn't an outright apology. That would have been better, but baby steps were good. With what was coming, it was better than nothing.

I stuffed the journal into the CVS bag and stepped out of Liz's car. The rain fell so hard and heavy, my shirt soaked through in seconds, but this was the first time I didn't mind. It was kind of beautiful living here with all the flowers, the perfectly manicured gardens, and hanging moss. I could understand why she liked it here, even if living in Savannah was like standing under a fire hose while trapped in an oven.

We ran under the awning of her building and up three flights of stairs. She turned the key in the lock. As we tumbled inside her apartment, it was dark for a moment, and my mind raced back to Castlebury's classroom. My heart thumped hard against my ribcage as Liz flipped the switch and the small living room came into focus. The Wraith wasn't here. I knew that logically, but for a second, I could have sworn something watched me.

"Are you okay?" Liz said. "You're clutching your heart like you're about to die."

I let go of my shirt. "Sorry," I said. "It was... scary, being in the dark."

My brain swam as I steadied myself on the brown, leather sofa. It was so old it really had no right to be anywhere but the dumpster, but Liz had kept it out of pure nostalgia. It used to sit in our parents' living room when we were small. The worn leather smell still reminded me of watching old movies, unwrapping presents, and having long conversations with my parents about school or friends. Now the couch lived here, a displaced memory, an artifact from another time. It belonged in the past, not here. Still, this piece of home was unexpectedly comforting as I tried to slow my frantic heartbeat.

Liz rung out her hair in the kitchen sink. "Do you feel up to eating some dinner? We have your favorite, leftover Hawaiian."

My stomach gave a sickening flop. "No. I just want to take a shower and go to bed."

"How about something to drink then?" She grabbed a cup, filled it up with water, and handed it to me before I could tell her no. "Gotta stay hydrated."

"Said like a true athlete," I said and took an obligatory sip, but it burned my throat. I had swallowed more smoke and ash than I realized. "Is there school tomorrow?"

She laughed. "Have class after an explosion? Ha! I don't think so. Why? Anxious to see your friends?"

I shrugged, fumbling for how to tell her I needed to see Marcus. "I don't know. I guess I'm worried about them. They got pretty hurt."

The leather creaked as she sat beside me. "Yeah you were asking about some guy named Marcus. Is he a... thing?"

I forced a laugh. "That guy? We are a thing precisely never. Not. Ever. If I lay dying in the middle of the street, I wouldn't ask him for a helping hand."

She smiled as her eyebrows raised. "Okay. You're not a thing. So...why care?"

My toes curled inside my dirty socks. I didn't know how to answer that. She wasn't wrong. I'd only known them for a day, but then I'd have to explain the Sparrows, Marcus, the Wraith, Dad, and everything else. When faced with the moment of actually telling her, I realized I wasn't ready at all. Maybe with eight hours of sleep I could take a stab at that five-hour long monologue. If I tried now with my body covered in blood and Wraith junk, I'd surely get every detail wrong. Then Liz would jump down my throat before thinking like always, and we'd be drawn even further apart.

When I didn't respond, she said, "Take a shower and go to bed. I have class, but you can take it easy. Sleep all day if you want. Watch some movies. Read some books or something. Stay offline. Don't drive yourself sick with worry."

"Oh, that will be easy," I said. "The, uh, electrical fire sort of destroyed my phone."

She sighed. "Well, that explains why you weren't getting any of my texts. We'll have to see if the insurance covers a new phone, but hey, new phone, am I right?"

She was being extraordinarily nice to me and it was super annoying. I expected her to be pissed I'd lost my phone, but here she was trying to be all chipper. After so much silence for so long, everything with Liz was forced and uncomfortable, like putting on shoes I had outgrown. I got up, leaving a small puddle of rainwater to pool in the sofa's cracks.

"And Jacks?" she said.

"Yeah?" I said over my shoulder, still heading to my bedroom.

"I know you don't want to," she said. "But you should talk about what happened. Don't bottle up your anger. It will eat you alive."

"Okay, okay. Fine." I gritted my teeth. "Just not right now. I'm so tired I'm going to faceplant into the carpet. First thing tomorrow. I promise."

"Okay," she said and watched me leave as I clicked the door shut behind me.

I flung the journal on my bed and paused when

I found my lamp was still on. The slow spin of the light through the cut-out constellations twirled around the bare room. Guess I forgot to turn it off. It was one of the few things I'd grabbed when Dad told me I was going to stay with Liz, one of the essentials. It wasn't a night light. Those were for children. It was a nostalgic source of light that helped me fall asleep.

Mom had given it to me, and even though the lamp was a source of comfort, looking at it was still a knife twist in my heart. Back when she was alive, we used to hold our arms open and spin. It was my favorite thing to do with my Mom when I was a kid. I would fall into the grass and the blue-black sky would roll with stars. She would laugh right next to me, our arms itching from the lawn and the mosquitos. She would tell me stories of Greek gods in the constellations and the dull world would stretch out into a mythic place. That's why she had bought it. She told me the light was meant to chase away the monsters, because when the stars were out, the night wasn't so scary. But now there were real monsters in the dark, and they knew where I hid. They would always know. Wherever I went, I was a beacon they would follow.

I peeled off my clothes and tossed them in the plastic hamper before heading into the small, private bathroom just off my bedroom. I turned the shower on hot, up near nuclear levels. A saltwater ocean smell hung heavy in the air. All of the water in the showers and sinks here stank like a crab-filled tide pool. Liz told me it was because we lived so close to the coast of Georgia. Every time I took a shower, I tried not to breathe in too deeply—another Savannah adjustment.

The heat helped scrub away the grime, but it still took three shampoos and most of a bar of soap to get rid of the penny smell of caked blood in my hair. The relief of being clean made me shiver. I washed everything five times, careful to ignore the stupid marks on my arms that shined much brighter in the water. First priority: Find Marcus and demand he give me the secret to nuking this gold mark right off my body. As much as I hated to admit it, I needed him. I had so many questions burning inside me. If I didn't talk to someone, anyone, I was going to explode.

Explode...Damn. Brent. Poor choice of words.

I scrubbed between my toes. Flakes of ash and little pieces of debris gathered at the bottom of the bathtub, gray like dead skin, like Bloody Mouth's face. It hadn't occurred to me until just then, but I was washing off pieces of Brent. *Oh God.* My stomach heaved and I coughed hard even though there was nothing in me to throw up.

I cut off the water. My legs shook as I stepped out of the tub. I wrapped myself in a fluffy towel, but I couldn't stop shaking. I tried putting my pajamas on and burying myself in my sheets, but my stupid hands would not stop trembling. It must be the exhaustion, not the people I killed today. Nope. Not that at all.

Who could I talk to? Liz was out. She couldn't even see the mark. Ashley was still in the hospital. I could call the school and get Marcus's address, but that was out too. There was no school anymore. I could Google him, find his Facebook. Where was my phone? *Damn.* I forgot again. I was so used to having my phone only a few inches away from my hand I didn't know what to do without it. My laptop was here, though. I'd brought it with me from home.

I reached for the computer bag beside my little twin bed and pulled it up to free my laptop. There wasn't a desk or any other furniture in this room after Liz's original roommate apparently bailed because this art school was so tough it was catastrophic to her health. I pulled out my older Mac, which was probably released around the time of the fourth or fifth iPhone, but it still got the job done. I logged into Facebook and searched for Marcus Blackwell and came up with nothing. I tried Instagram, Twitter, even Tumblr, and turned up exactly nothing. Who wasn't on social media? The guy was basically nonexistent. Maybe he was part of the mass exodus of people leaving because being on social media 24/7 was a drain on anyone's brain.

I Googled his name and found a shop called Blackwell Antiques in Savannah over on River Street. It wasn't too far to walk from here. I could hop over there and back before Liz even noticed I was gone. There were articles after the first link. I scrolled through their headlines.

"Notorious Ghost-Hunting Family Busted for False Ghost Claims."

"Blackwell's Caught in Shady Antique Deals. Close Shop to Public."

"One of Savannah's Oldest Families Steps Back from Limelight After Public Scandal."

So that's why Becky didn't want to be associated with the Blackwells. Their public image was absolutely horrible. I checked Google Maps to see if their store was still there. Their shop was still over on River Street. It was worth checking out, even if it was shut down.

I closed my laptop. *What would Mom do if she were here?*

The question surprised me. I'm not sure why it had bubbled up in my thoughts. I pictured her hard, gray eyes. She was the most skeptical person I'd ever known. She was always in a state of low-key rage and defensiveness, except for when she looked at us, her girls. Mom wore her anger like battle armor, living as if she were constantly ready for an attack. After today, I guess I didn't wonder why anymore. These ghosts and demons must have been chasing her for her whole life, but as I grew up, I never saw a single ghost. I reached for the journal without thinking and opened a random page to a bit of torn paper taped inside.

Savannah, Georgia, is considered one of the

most haunted cities in the United States. In its downtown historical area, nearly every building claims a recurring haunting. This has driven massive amounts of tourists to the area and provided a sizable portion of the city's overall income.

Once a prominent seafaring trade route since its establishment in 1733, the amount of supernatural activity is long associated with several historical events, such as Oglethorpe's landing and multiple buildings positioned over several burial grounds. It is also attributed to the number of headstones that were relocated when General Sherman marched through Savannah, never to be returned to their original lots. Whatever the case, it is historically acknowledged that Savannah is a city built on its dead.

- Article Clipping from "Savannah, A Haunted History" by Dr. Henry Fitzgerald, PHD

I slammed the journal shut and threw the stupid book against the wall. It landed with a dull thud before flopping onto my dirty laundry, but I didn't care. *Savannah is one of the most haunted cities in America.* Dad knew. He absolutely knew. He was a historical journalist for the university. Marcus was right—Dad left me in the worst possible place, knowing full-well the demons were going to come. The betrayal flooded through me in waves. I wanted to scream or cry or throw more books, but there was nothing left inside of me, nothing but cold.

Goddamnit Dad.

"Sparrow."

My body went rigid.

No. It couldn't be.

The Wraith was dead.

I got up from my bed and shuffled across the room to part the blinds with my finger. The rain had stopped, and the clouds had retreated, revealing a waxing moon. Moss swayed from the branches of the oak just outside the window, like little ghosts in the moonlight. Crickets and frogs sang in a musical hum. I listened to the sounds of the night, more apparent now that the rain had stopped. Maybe I had finally snapped, or maybe my mind was echoing the events from earlier today because I was too tired to function.

My hands. No electricity. It seemed to only happen whenever demons were around, or times of high stress. If the Wraith had returned, my body would know, like a personal alarm system complete with light show.

I waited for a long time, enough for my feet to go numb and my neck to go stiff from my tense shoulders. As I stumbled back into the bedroom and face-planted into bed, I pushed down the watery anxiety. Nothing was coming to get me. Processing the journal and Dad's epic betrayal would have to wait. I closed my eyes and all I saw were images of the Wraith. I kept reliving the sensation of my fingers against Brent as he

Lady of
Bone

Lady of
Shadow

Lady of
Blood

Three Sisters

I have to get Emily out of here.

They've got some sort of plan for her and her sister. I overheard Arturo talking with his wife Miriam about new ways of forcing the sisters to combine their powers to create something called the Mirror Door. Emily is afraid of what she'll let through, what she will give a body, if she calls on her power again. We need to get out, but Amelia doesn't want to leave. She believes their best chance is to stay and learn how to control their gifts under Arturo, but she's wrong. Arturo wants to use them. He doesn't care about keeping people safe like he claims. He wants something more, something personal. I think he believes Emily and Amelia can open a door to the other side, but what for? If that happens, Emily thinks she and her sister will disappear. Every time they force her to use her powers, the mark grows. I don't know what it means, but it can't be good.

Jacob
March 1, 1991

7

Run

"SPARROW."

I blinked awake. The room was dark. Too dark. My heart pounded inside my chest as I realized the lamp had stopped spinning. Normally, the stars would sweep around the room across posters of all the places I wanted to travel when I graduated high school. Only, this wasn't my bedroom and I wasn't back home, and the lamp sat there like a broken toy in the spare room of my sister's apartment with its bare, white walls.

I reached out. My fingers cramped as if winter had just breathed across my skin. Impossible. It was almost summer. Maybe the air conditioning unit under the window was broken. I pushed off the sheets, making a leap for my robe hanging on the back of the door. The carpet was so cold it pricked my feet. I slipped on the robe, but it did absolutely nothing to warm me. I waved a hand over the air conditioning unit and it whirred pleasant balmy air against my fingertips. Only one thing could make the room this cold, and it was in the apartment with me.

A noise came from the other side of my bedroom door. It clattered and slammed, clattered, and slammed, as if someone were opening and shutting the kitchen silverware drawer. No. It couldn't be the Wraith. Bloody Mouth was dead. I glanced at Dad's journal, which was still resting all crumpled and neglected on top of the hamper where I had thrown it before I fell asleep. I picked it up by the spine and flipped open the pages but couldn't tell one entry from another in the dark. *Where is that Banishment ward?*

I tried flicking the bedroom light switch on. Nothing. I reached for my dresser drawer and pulled out the flashlight Liz gave me for emergencies. Dad was the one who started calling her "Safety First Liz" or "Operation Preparation." For the first time ever, I was grateful she was the most Girl Scout person on Earth. The light came on and illuminated the pages. I flipped to the section with the Banishment symbol. If it worked on the Wraith before, it could work again. I held the book out like a shield in front of me as I approached the bedroom door.

The clanging stopped. Little currents of blue light snaked up the back of my fingers as I held the flashlight, causing the bulb to flicker. Something was definitely out there. My power knew it, I knew it, but what was out there?

The brass handle turned all on its own. The flashlight blinked rapidly in my hand as I shoved the book out in front of me like a shield. The bedroom door swung open with a creaky whine and stopped. I listened. There was nothing but the sound of my own breathing. The living room stretched out like a massive black hole in front of me. I had to take care of this entity myself, but go out there? Alone? That option was a great big old pile of *nope*. I pointed my flashlight into the gloom, but it was like trying to shine a light into a giant storm cloud.

"I know you're out there." I whispered. "I know what you want."

Metal scraped across metal in the direction of the kitchen. Something fluttered against my back. My bedroom door slammed shut behind me. I dropped the flashlight and velvety darkness soaked the world around me. I grasped around the carpet. *Crap. Crap. CRAP.* Something hard and heavy collided with my calves. The journal went flying as I face-planted into the floor.

It pressed down in the center of my back, like someone dropped a stack of gym weights on me. My arms flailed around the carpet to push myself up, but it was so heavy, I couldn't bend my elbows enough to lift. The pressure increased and I choked as my spine sank down against my rib cage. My legs and arms flailed. I clawed, struggling for air.

My body flopped once and then went completely still. The weight released. I could breathe, but the pressure was still there, crushing down inside my ribcage instead of on top of my skin. There came a whoosh of air and my skin pricked all over as if I'd just been hit by a gust of snow. I instinctively raised my arms to block the wind from my face, but they didn't respond. My arms wouldn't move. My fingers, my toes, my legs—I tried anything, everything. Nothing in my body was mine.

My right arm lifted gently, but the sensation was distant from my mind, my control. I felt it happening, but I wasn't doing it. My left arm lifted, and I found myself on my knees, but I hadn't put myself there. I screamed inside my body, but my mouth didn't so much as twitch. My body was a cage, and I was trapped inside.

My hands reached up and around behind me. My back arched as my body bent in two and lifted off the floor. Hair dangled in front of my face as I floated up to the ceiling. Tears itched the top of my eyelids. Warm liquid trickled down between my legs and little droplets hit the carpet below. Tears ran over my forehead and into my hair.

In the warm pit of my stomach, something wiggled around like a snake. It crawled out of the base of my spine, slithered up and out of my throat, and spoke using my mouth.

"Possessing you was too easy," my voice said.

Hearing myself say the words drowned all the hope inside of me. This is what happened to Brent, what it felt like. It could have possessed Liz to get to me, could have taken anyone, but it had chosen me. I had my answer. A ghost did not need a host to attack me. Whatever possessed me was definitely a demon, but was it the Wraith?

"I thought the great Sparrow would be difficult." My tongue licked my lips, as if the demon found the ability to use my mouth absolutely delicious. *"You are as weak as all the rest. You have power, a great deal of it, but you are not invincible."*

No. You're wrong. I thought what I wanted to say as hard as I could. *I'm not weak, Wraith. I'm not powerless. My body is mine.*

"But I'm not a Wraith," I whispered like a lover. Static danced across my arms in little arcs of blue lightning and my eyes widened. *"What power,"* my voice said with such awe.

I calmed my mind and searched for where the demon hid inside me. A lump of ice rested at the base of my spine. *Gotcha.* My power uncoiled and focused in on the little chunk of cold and drew it out, like pulling venom from a snake bite. My body slammed against the ceiling. I crawled in circles around the metal fan, my knees scraping against the rough patches of uneven plaster.

"Don't," my voice hissed. *"If you try to remove me, I'll use your power right now and give myself a body. And then where would you*

be?"

I knew exactly where. In pieces all over the floor. If I used my Summoning gift to get rid of the demon, I would have no choice but to give it a body. I would be torn apart, just like Brent. How in the hell was I going to get this thing out of me?

The journal. It was still lying on the floor, face up and open to the symbol page. If I could get to it, maybe I could use one of the wards against it. Hell, I'd even roll my body over the symbols if that's what it took to get the demon out. Here's hoping whatever was currently using me for puppet practice fell under the category of "lesser demons."

Hey, demon. I thought it as hard as I could. *You see that book?*

My head turned towards Dad's journal. **"Yes...I see the primitive infernal architecture you call demonic symbology. It won't work. Not on me. I can hear your thoughts, Sparrow. You can't hide your plans from me. There's nothing you can do to make me touch that book."**

Damn. New plan. I couldn't think of a plan while trying to make the plan, or it would hear me. I needed something better, something unexpected, something...

Liz's bedroom door flew open. "What the actual hell?"

She had a softball bat cocked in both hands ready to swing, the one she used to use back in

If I could
This was
pect—an

ice hissed.

's across
itchen. I
over the
ghtened
nd closed
und the
wall and
r feet as

ny mind.
ed!
ed.
ld lump
of Liz?
her grip
ne? Liz
hed the
suck out
around

th said.
er will

iz said.

the kitchen floor.
like I'd just cough
"Liz?" My voice
me."
"Oh my God, J
quick as a blown—
her arms. "It's yo
I wept into her
My arms were mi
I cried because I
sob into my siste
"Two Sparro
me there was o
Liz yanked m
gelatin quivered
The horrible ma
beach ball. Two
inspect us. Fing
tree parted the
giant, black ballo
dancer, stretche
nostrils and a wi
gunk. The long
face from its chi
the size of penc
other with chat
blob lifted and c
kitchen. Despit
it was still tran
onto the floor. I
journal. It was t

high school when she made varsity. If I could have grinned ear-to-ear, I would have. This was exactly what the demon would never expect—an angry, bat-wielding Liz.

"Your bleeding girl is mine," my voice hissed. *"You shall not have her."*

My body scurried away on all fours across the ceiling into the sanctuary of the kitchen. I climbed and hid in the dark shadow over the laundry room door, perched like a frightened spider. The cabinet doors flapped open and closed beneath me in warning. The chairs around the kitchen table slid out and flew into the wall and sofa. Liz leapt away from the lamp by her feet as the light surged and the bulb popped.

"What is happening?"

Come on, Liz. I reached out to her in my mind. *Figure it out. Make the leap. I'm possessed!*

"Don't touch me!" the demon shrieked.

Inside the pit of my stomach, the cold lump shuddered. Why was the demon so afraid of Liz? Her wide eyes narrowed as she renewed her grip on the bat. Did she actually just hear me? Liz took one step at a time as she approached the kitchenette, where all the light seemed to suck out of the air around me. My hand wrapped around my throat and squeezed.

"Come any closer, Sparrow," my mouth said. *"And I'll release myself and your sister will die to make way for my birth."*

"I don't know what the hell you are," Liz said.

"But I've seen the Exorcist and I know how this works. You're not my sister. You're something else."

Sparrow? Why did it just call Liz the Sparrow?

Liz raised the bat. "Get the hell out of my sister!"

Every kitchen cabinet door opened at once. Plates slid off their shelves and took flight, aiming themselves at Liz. She swung her bat, shattering as many as she could. She dodged bowls as they flung themselves at her head. The demon groaned as my finger pointed at the drawer full of silverware and it slammed open. The forks, spoons, and knives stood up on end. I laughed deep and horrible, but the voice was no longer in my mouth. It was all around me yet far away, like an echo off a mountain top.

Blue light winked around my hands, so hot, too hot. My lips parted and gritty smoke billowed out of my mouth like a swarm of flies. It was coming. This was it, the moment the demon used my power to give itself a body. The cold lump inside pressed on my lungs as it grew.

"No, you don't." Liz leapt for me. With a twist of her hand, she yanked me down by my shirt.

The demon screamed as my body crashed onto the linoleum and broken plates. She held onto my waist as I bucked away from her grip. My feet swatted broken porcelain in every direction. Liz yanked my hair back to force my body to still. I spit at her and a little glob of black landed on her eye and dribbled down. She wiped it away, disgusted, and pinned my arms back.

The cold pit inside me writhed and burned. *"What are you doing?"*

She held me fast. "You're getting out of my sister, and you're getting out now."

Light curled at the end of Liz's fingertips, but it wasn't blue like mine. It was green as a field in spring. The air smelled warm and wet, like freshly churned earth, like morning dew on a cut lawn. Liz looked down at her fingers and gaped. Beads of sweat formed on her forehead as she paled.

"What?" She slowly released a breath as the green light in her hands grew, observing her power with a gentle awe.

"Do not touch me, Sparrow," it said. *"Keep away."*

Liz, the Sparrow? But she can't be. She had never manifested at the right age, but the proof was undeniable. Her light blazed as she pressed her hands against my chest. This was it. This was how I died. I braced myself for the end, waited for my body to burst, waited for the last thing I saw to be the demon ripping out of me. It was all so unexpectedly...calm. The green light of her power washed over me like hot, summer wind across a hill. This didn't feel like my power. It was something different, something gentle. If this was how I died, at least it was peaceful.

I rolled over and threw up a black blob onto

the kitchen floor. Everything felt hot and cold, like I'd just coughed up the remnants of a bad flu.

"Liz?" My voice trembled. "It's me. I swear it's me."

"Oh my God, Jacks!" Her light snuffed out, quick as a blown-out candle, and she took me in her arms. "It's you. It's really you."

I wept into her shoulder as she cradled my head. My arms were mine and my legs were mine and I cried because I didn't know what else to do but sob into my sister's arms.

"Two Sparrows," a voice said. ***"They told me there was only one."***

Liz yanked me away from the blob. The gelatin quivered as it spread out into a puddle. The horrible mass swelled up, rounding into a beach ball. Two little white beads poked out to inspect us. Fingers as delicate as the roots on a tree parted the slime as it filled the room like a giant, black balloon. Two arms, slender as a ballet dancer, stretched out of the glob. A face with two nostrils and a wide mouth emerged from the shiny gunk. The long mouth spread up, splitting its face from its chin to its forehead. Slender teeth the size of pencil erasers ground against each other with chattering pleasure. The demonic blob lifted and came to float in the center of the kitchen. Despite how thick and shiny it seemed; it was still transparent as globs of filth dripped onto the floor. I'd seen a drawing of it in Dad's journal. It was the worst page in the entire book.

The Poltergeist.

"No matter," it said as it tapped its fingertips together in endless impatience. **"I only need the Sparrow of Summoning."**

"Jacks." Liz reached for the bat. "Get behind me."

I grabbed her arm. "Don't do this. It's a Poltergeist. It will suck you in. There's no beating it."

"On the count of three, run." Her grip on the bat tightened, and the demon hissed between its long teeth. "One."

"Don't do this," I said, yanking her arm. "We have to go! Now!"

The demon's fingers thump-thumped, thump-thumped as it hovered closer to Liz. **"Interesting. You reach for your mortal weapon but not the one inside you. You do not know who you are."**

Liz ignored the demon and shook me off of her. She took the bat in both hands as she came to her feet. "Two."

She didn't wait for the count of three. She slammed the baseball bat into the side of the Poltergeist's massive head. It landed with a thick, wet *smack*, as if she'd hit a pound of clay.

"An interesting game," the demon said as it twisted its neck to look at her. Liz yanked at the bat to strike again, but it stayed fixed in the goo. **"I will devour you first, Sparrow of Banishment."**

Sparrow of Banishment? Marcus's words came rushing back to me, the strange quip he made while grabbing my face: *"You are the Sparrow. But not the competent one, not the one who banishes instead of summoning."*

"Liz!" I said. "You have to banish it!"

"What the hell are you talking about?" Liz tugged at the bat again, but it wouldn't come loose.

"That isn't going to work. Do it again!" I said. "Call the light that comes out of your hands and send it packing!"

Sinews of glossy flesh leapt from the demon's chest and snaked to latch onto Liz's hands. "It burns!" Her voice trembled as she screamed. "Oh my God, get it off!"

She clawed the demon to pry herself away, but the living ink snatched her free hand. It pulled and Liz sank all the way up to her elbow. The Poltergeist was going to devour her. She was too afraid to use her power. In a few more seconds, my sister would be gone.

The Summoning power filled my chest with warmth and light, rushed out from my core and flooded down my arms. My fingertips buzzed with pressure. I had to do something, but my gift was useless. It only killed people. As I wrestled with what to do, I couldn't stop wondering why I had been so mad at her. I was so stuck on believing she didn't want me here, but that wasn't true. As my sister sank into the black mud, fire bubbled up in the pit of my stomach. I couldn't lose her.

Not ever again.

Lightning danced in my vision and spread across my chest, but this time it wasn't blue. The summoning had turned a violent shade of reddish gold. My mouth gaped as my legs shook with a strange weakness, as if I'd just run ten miles. The feeling of summoning was so different than before, strangely more natural than the Wraith.

Do it. Just let go.

Think how much better you'll feel if you just let go.

I reached for the Poltergeist.

"Don't!" Liz said. "It will suck you in too. Just leave me."

Red light spilled from my hands and bloomed inside me like a flower opening to the night. "No. I'm not leaving you," I said. "I'm never going to leave you ever again."

Gold electricity crackled across the kitchen, so bright I couldn't see. My hands buzzed as the floodgates inside me unlatched. I smiled, closed my eyes, and let go.

8

Cost

RED AND GOLD LIGHTNING spilled out of my hands and into the demon. My whole body buzzed, electrified with meaning and happiness as I sent everything I had into the Poltergeist. The gold mark danced as if my body were fashioned out of roaring flames. The demon shrank away from Liz as it tried to release her in order to flee from me, but it was stuck in its own disgusting muck.

"Stop, Sparrow!" Its screech was the awful high pitch of a drowning rat. *"Don't do this! It's too much power. Don't—"*

Liz screamed as the demon burst in her hands. A bubble of ash and muck exploded across the kitchen and slapped me in the face. I wiped away the debris and spit out a grisly black piece that tasted like rotten eggs. As my heart slowed, the sensation under my skin retreated, but my soul sang. I resisted. I hadn't given the demon a body—I had destroyed it.

I stumbled into the sink and grabbed the counter as my head swam in the turbulent sea of my emotions. "Whoa," I said. "I can't believe I did that."

Liz didn't acknowledge me. She stood there, face covered in sludge, and stared with a kind of absence that scared me. She was always prepared for everything, but nothing could have prepared her for this.

I touched her shoulder. "Liz?"

Her eyes were vacant. "What...happened?"

"Hey, it's going to be okay." I wiped away as much of the grit as I could from her face, enough to reveal her freckled cheeks. "It's gone now."

Liz leaned over the sink and vomited.

"See that was my reaction the first time, too," I said as I rubbed her back and she threw up everything she had. It should have completely disgusted me, but all I felt was relief. I could explode demons, which was kind of a cool power to have. The next time one of them came around, all I had to do was explode them. It was all so simple, except that it really wasn't. Doing that had left me weaker than a newborn kitten. I didn't think I could do that again without passing out.

Liz wiped her mouth with the back of her hand and turned around. Her hands trembled as she pointed to something behind me. "Jacks. It's coming back."

The bits of demon splattered around the kitchen crawled across the linoleum. They inched along the countertops and down the cabinets to join in the gathering blob on the floor.

"Damnit." My voice shook just as much as hers did. "I don't think I can get rid of them. You're going to have to use your power this time."

She shook her head so hard I worried it would fall right off her neck. "No. I'm not touching that thing."

I took her by her shoulders and gave her a firm shake. "Listen to me. Don't look at that thing. Remember the lights? The ones in your hands you used to get the demon out of me. You have a gift. I know you feel really hesitant to call for it to come out, but you're going to have to do it right now."

"Demon? What?" Liz shut her eyes tight. "This isn't happening."

"I swear it is," I said. "And if you don't release right now this thing is going to possess me again. It's a demon called a Poltergeist, but it wants a body, and I have this power where I can give it one. It will possess me again if you don't call on what's sleeping inside of you to banish it. *Please.* What I did wasn't enough. I can't banish it. Only you can."

"Okay." She opened her eyes. "I'll try."

The demon stretched its arms out of the muck,

re-growing its limbs. Its smiled widened as its two beady little eyes saw and understood we were floundering. ***"Sparrows..."*** it crooned. ***"Oh, little Sparrows..."***

I swallowed hard. "Do you remember that feeling when the green light came? Search your body. Do you feel it in your stomach?"

She shook her head. "It's not in my stomach. It's in my chest."

I grabbed her by the shoulders and pushed her towards the demon. "Call that light again and send it into the Poltergeist."

The demon's arms reached for us as both of Liz's arms ignited. Emerald fire wrapped around her body, so bright I couldn't see. She screamed as the demon burned away, as bits of it fell apart and floated away to ash in her hands. There was a thunderclap followed by a percussive gust of air that blew my hair back, and the demon was gone. The kitchen filled with a rotten egg smell so strong I gagged.

Liz swatted the smell away. "God, that stinks."

I jumped up and down. "You did it! I can't believe you did it!"

Liz laughed a little too hard. "Oh my God, that just came out of me! I was like whoosh and then there was a pop and it was gone!" She arched her hands and punched, recreating the drama blow-by-blow.

"I know!" My voice was excited but weary. "I can't believe it."

"That was insane!" she giggled. "I fought it and it came back and I burst with fire and wow! I had no idea I could do something like that. I can't believe demons are *real*."

I nodded as the linoleum swam under me. My butt hit the counter as I slid down to the kitchen floor.

She held a hand out to me. "Are you okay?"

I nodded as I reached for her. "Yeah. Just a little dizzy."

She pulled her hand away from me, face pale.

"What is it?" I said.

"Your arms..." she said.

The mark was above my elbows now, glittering like opera gloves. I swallowed hard. Guess I couldn't hide it anymore. She had woken up. I hung my head.

"You asked me to tell you what happened at school," I said. "But it started back in Atlanta. A ghost attacked me during volleyball practice. Dad was there. He saved me. That night, he told me he wanted to bring me here, to you. He told me he'd only be gone for a little while. He needed to search Savannah for something stronger to protect me. Remember that crystal necklace Mom always wore? The pink one?"

She didn't say anything, but her eyes were very wide and very wet. I kept talking. "Dad said it would repel anything supernatural, but it didn't work. The demon found me anyway." The knees of my pajama pants turned wet with my tears.

"Yesterday, at Northwinds, a demon called the Wraith came to my Biology class and possessed a guy named Brent. It used him to try to kill me, and I defended myself. I accidentally touched Brent and the demon... well, the demon ripped right out of him."

Liz crossed her arms as she leaned against the stove. "So, what you're saying is... you killed him."

I buried my head against my knees and made my voice as small as possible. "Yes."

"And just now, another demon came," she said. "They want you to give them a body, and they're probably going to keep coming, aren't they?"

"Yes." I wiped my eyes on the back of my hand. "And every time I use my power, the mark grows. It's equivalent exchange. You know, *'to take something out, something must be put back.'* To give a body, I have to give some of mine."

She let out a long breath. "And what happens when you've run out of body to give?"

I sighed. "I don't know. Marcus said I'm being pulled into this place called the Other, but I haven't been able to find him since the attack to figure out where that is."

Her eyes lit up. "So that's why you were wondering where he was back at the hospital. Who is he?"

I snorted. "I don't know. Some guy in my class who knows way too much about demons, and about Sparrows. He was kind of a jerk to me, acting all superior because I didn't know what was happening. It's not like Dad told me."

Liz's eyes widened as she processed. "Dad didn't tell you anything?"

I rolled my eyes. "That's the worst part. He not only told us precisely nothing, Dad *knew* there was a chance we might become Sparrows during our teenage years. He knew Savannah was haunted as hell, but he just shoved his journal and was like "figure it out." Then he rushed off to find something called the Obsidian necklace that supposedly works way better than the garbage necklace Mom had."

"The rose quartz," she nodded, still processing. "It's a symbol of love and protection, especially when given by someone who loved you. Maybe that's what Dad thought it would do—protect you with Mother's love. Obsidian is a powerful shield, which makes sense. Wearing it, you'd be invisible to anything that wished you harm."

I blinked at her. "Wow. I had no idea you knew so much."

"I studied crystals for an art project," she said, shrugging it off. "So, he left you here to find a more powerful necklace. What happened to Mom's?"

I kicked away a broken piece of plate and it skidded across the kitchen. "It broke the second the Wraith attacked. I was frustrated. I just sort of left it there."

She nodded vaguely and looked away from me, somehow hurt that I'd leave Mom's necklace like that. I glanced at my arms. They glittered in the morning light that peeked between the blinds in the living room. "Listen, Dad told me you didn't have any powers, to keep you out of it. I didn't know this would happen. I swear I didn't. If I thought they would come for me, I would have told you."

Her voice was as hollow and empty as her face. "I know." She turned away from me, crossed the kitchen over to the sink, and started scrubbing her arms like a robot. "How long have you had your power?"

I shrugged. "Since Tuesday. The day before Dad brought me here. Not long at all. Why?"

Liz sighed. "That lines up with what happened to me. I thought I'd dreamt it, but I guess I didn't. Two nights ago, I woke to the sound of fingers tapping on my bedroom window. I opened the curtain. A woman floated outside my window. There was a black ribbon wrapped around her neck. She put a finger to her lips, like she wanted me to be quiet, and then she pulled end of the ribbon. Her head came tumbling off her neck." She closed her eyes and exhaled long and slow. "I threw my arms up to defend myself and saw a green light. Then, she was gone. I didn't know what happened, but I guess I *banished* her." She shut off the water and dried her hands on a paper towel, her way of saying she was done talking.

"That is truly haunting," I said. "It sounds like we woke up on the same day. I don't know why, but I think I know where we can find some answers. Like I said, Dad left me a journal, but I haven't had a chance to read it cover-to-cover."

"Let's read it together, but first, I desperately need a shower." She grabbed her shirt and wrung it out as she walked into the disaster area that was her living room. Bits of blood and chunks of bone fell into the squishy black pile on the floor. "I think I will need to bathe for the next ten years before I'll feel clean again."

"Liz?" I said, "are you...mad at me for not telling you?"

"There will be no cleaning this." She sighed as she surveyed her destroyed apartment. "I wanted to be mad. I really, *really* wanted to hate you for keeping secrets from me, but then I thought about it. You tried to tell me at breakfast, didn't you?"

"Yeah," I said. "I tried, but...you left before I could explain."

"And I'm the one who blew you off." She picked the lamp up off the floor and placed it back on side table. "If there's anyone I'm mad at, it's Dad, not you. He didn't tell either of us anything. He could have told us something, anything, but he didn't."

I stared at the sludge caking her arms and my stomach tightened. She was being surprisingly okay with all of this. I raised an eyebrow at her. "You sure you're fine? You're being remarkably chill about all of this."

She attempted to give me a genuine smile. "You're right. I'm barely hanging on, to be honest.

Besides, we've both been attacked enough for one day. I don't feel like fighting anymore."

I smiled as my shoulders relaxed. It felt so good to have someone who understood what I was going through, but most of all, it was wonderful that person was my sister. When Mom died, she'd been lost to me, and after a while I thought she would never come back. On my own it would be impossible to keep outrunning these things while I played the waiting game for Dad to come back, but with Liz we'd not only be able to fight; we'd be able to *win*.

She walked out of the kitchen and into the living room, surveyed the destroyed dishes and silverware spread across the carpet from my bedroom to hers, and groaned. "There is no way I'm going to feel safe sleeping here. Besides, the apartment is trashed. We can't stay. The woman with the ribbon, that Poltergeist, they found us here and more will come. Let's get a hotel and crash and figure out a plan from there. Dad left me a credit card. Let him deal with the situation he's put us in. Let's grab a shower. Meet back here in twenty?"

"Sure," I said, feeling more optimism than I had in the past forty-eight hours. "That sounds like a plan."

Liz headed into her room and shut the door behind her with a gentle click. The sun had risen while we debated, and orange light peeked through the blinds across the sofa and carpet. It wasn't night anymore. It was morning. I'd barely slept.

I groaned as I inspected the Poltergeist residue that clumped in little pieces all over my body and forced the little hairs on the back of my arms to stick together. *Gross. Why do these stupid demons insist on trashing everything around them?* I staggered out of the living room and into the shower, forcing myself to stay under the hot water for as long as I could stand it. I scrubbed a bit, but it didn't make a difference. The collective sludge from the Wraith and the "Goth Pudding" Poltergeist were probably never fully leaving my hair. I'd have better luck shaving my head.

I got out of the shower, changed, and packed all of my things into my duffle bag as fast as possible. The last thing to go in was Dad's journal, which I did not want to stick with my clean clothes and computer. It still smelled like soggy pennies and gutter water. I flipped open the book, searching for the page of the demon we'd just fought. I found the right page pretty quick.

"So, I was right. It was a Poltergeist," I said out loud to myself because I was not a crazy person. "Mom, you did your best, but you could not capture just how disgusting that demon was in real life."

I tucked the journal under my arm, making a mental note to share it with Liz when we got to the hotel, and took one last look at the room. I'd left the constellation lamp on the table. It was the only thing of mine I'd left behind in the entire room. I turned on my heel, not caring what happened to it anymore. It wouldn't protect me any more than Mom's necklace had.

POLTERGEIST

What have I done?

The test ritual was a success. Emily and Amelia created the Mirror Door, a small gateway to the Other. I watched from the hall, hiding to make sure nothing happened to Emily. He praised them, said this was but a small step to the greatest feat of all—the opening of the Black Gate. Emily refused to open it. Amelia begged her to do what he said, fearing Arturo. He backhanded Emily and called her horrible things, claiming he was the only thing that kept their powers from destroying every last living person on Earth. I couldn't stand it anymore. I took his knife and did what had to be done.

I didn't hear Emily crying until it was over, until Arturo was lying on the floor covered in blood and my hands were filthy and the room smelled like his death. I dropped his salt knife. All I wanted was to help Emily escape. I never meant to kill anyone. Miriam found us leaving as she was coming home. She ran inside the house. Emily, Amelia and I ran as fast and hard as we could, but we could not outrun Miriam's gun.

Jacob
March 23, 1991

9

Pieces

LIZ GRIPPED THE WHEEL of the Honda as it careened down the road. The gold markings on my hands twinkled, bright and unnatural in the early morning light. I balled my fists inside the sleeves of my hoodie. The sooner I found Marcus and demand he somehow get rid of the equivalent exchange mark, the better.

I wiped my sleeve across the glass to clear the fog that had accumulated from last night's rain. The Honda buzzed past red brick buildings, shops and restaurants, apartments, and pharmacies. Out my window, people lounged at tables in little cafes, drank coffee and read books. I envied their ability to relax, to act normal. Even as light filtered between the hanging moss and cast small rainbows on the pink azaleas below, I couldn't feel safe. It felt like all of Savannah had eyes, and the city itself was watching me.

Liz pulled off and slid into an open spot on the street in front of a giant red brick building with dozens of windows and a front porch that stretched the length of it. The sign read: Marshall House.

"This looks good," Liz said. "What do you think?"

"This place? Really?" I asked. "It looks...pricey."

She put the car in park. "I need somewhere within walking distance of my classes and this is on the same road as Jen Library, where I need to be later this afternoon. Just go inside and see if they have something available."

I fidgeted with my seatbelt. "Book a hotel room? Me? I have zero idea how. Besides, odds are good they won't let a fifteen-year-old girl who doesn't even have a learner's permit book a room. How is this in any way a good plan?"

I wanted to go on lecturing her, but Liz had rested her head against the steering wheel. Her cheeks were so pale her freckles were almost translucent. She didn't look good at all.

"Please," she said between breaths. "Do this for me. All I need is for you to ask if they have availability. I'll be inside in a minute."

I rubbed her back. "Are you okay?"

"Not really," she said. "Banishing that demon took a lot out of me. If I get some sleep before class, I'll be fine."

"You're not seriously thinking of going back to school with potentially every demon and ghost in Savannah out to get us?"

She laughed a little. "I know they're scary and all, but honestly...I fear my college professors more."

I laughed. "Your teachers are scarier than the parade of disgusting demons trying to attack us every five minutes? I seriously doubt that." I unbuckled my seatbelt, stuffed the journal into my duffle bag, and climbed out of the car. "Don't worry. I'll take care of the room. Meet me inside when you can."

I shut the car door behind me, headed up the porch steps, and marched through the green double doors of Marshall House.

Well. Crap.

If I thought Northwinds was posh as hell, Marshall House was ten billion times worse. The gold wallpaper, marble and cherry-wood tables, and plush leather chairs were arranged as if they were set up for a photoshoot in *Southern Living* magazine. Huge floral bouquets adorned all the tables with fragrant, pink peonies and delicate, white feverfew daisies. Paintings of farms and plantations hung over a dimly lit sitting area with a fireplace near a brass and granite bar. A majestic staircase with plush red carpet led to another level.

How in the hell were we going to afford this?

Correction: How in the hell was Dad going to be able to afford this?

I rang the bell. A man wearing a button-down shirt and a beard that hung over his belly came to sit on a bar stool behind the counter. His tiny round glasses and mustache that curled up at both ends made me think more of a steampunk aeronaut than a hotel manager. When he smiled, it was unexpectedly pleasant. His name tag read *Gary*.

"Do you have a room available?" I asked, trying to make my voice sound commanding.

He looked me up and down, eyes narrow. "For yourself?"

"For my sister and I," I said and gave my best smile. "She's sick in the car."

He leaned his giant forearms across the counter and looked me up and down again. "You sure you two are old enough to be stayin' without an adult? You don't look it to me. Wouldn't be comfortable letting you stay if your folks didn't know where you were."

Damn. That's the thing about the South. People wanted to know your business forever and always, and they wouldn't stop being prying jerks. Time to be bold. What would Liz do?

I stood a little straighter. "I don't know what business it is of yours what our situation is or why we need a room. I'm simply checking to see if one is available while she parks the car, and if you can't help us, we will kindly take our business elsewhere and give you a scathing review shout-out to our ample social media accounts."

That last part was a lie, but it was all I could think of on the spot.

He sighed, settled back in his creaking chair. "I meant no disrespect. I just wanted to be sure you two weren't in some kind of...situation you didn't want to be in. If you *do* need help, if someone is giving you trouble, I'm happy to give a call to the proper authorities."

A blush flooded my face as I remembered the scar on my cheek from the glass cut. It hadn't occurred to me that Gary might think we were running away from a tough situation at home, and that was how I got this particular cut to the face. Actual kindness from a stranger wasn't even on my radar. Most of the time back home, people were nice and smiled to your face, but if you weren't kin or a really close friend, they wouldn't lift a finger to help you if you were lying bleeding in the street. But there were those who were genuinely kind, and Gary's kindness reminded me not everything fell under my cynical radar.

"Sorry," I said. "It's been a long night. We're fine, it's just—" I paused and thought for a moment. "Our apartment flooded."

"I see," Gary said and then typed something on his computer. "How many?"

I leaned on the counter. "Two people, like I said."

"No," he said slowly. "I mean nights. How many

nights will you be staying?"

I twisted my hair so hard a strand broke. *Why did you have to leave me with the difficult part, Liz? I don't know how many nights!* I leaned to check out the glass double doors to see if Liz was coming to rescue me. She was still resting her face on the steering wheel. She really *was* sick.

I let go of my hair and put my hands down by my sides. "Three nights."

He typed again. "Room 316 is available. You let me know if your plans change. I'll keep the room open for you. Just need a photo ID, credit card for the deposit, and we're all set."

Damn. I'd completely forgotten to ask Liz for the card. My lips pressed together. She'd acted so nonchalant about using it. Dad left her one of his credit cards, sure, but he was broker than broke.

"Let me get my sister," I said. He agreed to watch my bag for me, so I left my duffle bag on the counter before heading back outside.

My trot over to the car made Liz lift her head enough to see me. She pressed the window button until it rolled all the way down. "Did you get the room?"

"Yes. He wants us to pay." I crossed my arms. "He also asked how long we were staying. I said three days."

"That's fine." She fished around in her duffle bag until she pulled out a wallet and a credit card with Dad's name on it. She handed it to me. "Go ahead and book it. I'll be right behind you."

I took the wallet and returned to Gary, who had apparently been watching us the whole time. He held out a hand and glanced at the name on the card.

"Jacob Strange," he said as he ran it through the chip reader.

"That's my Dad." I shifted from foot to foot, praying the card would go through.

Gary's smile was thin as he handed me the card along with our room keys. "Everything checked out. Rate's usually $260 a night, but I'm going to give you a discount. You'll see that come out on the card when you leave. Complimentary breakfast until ten AM."

I let out a quiet exhale as I took the card. "Thank you so much."

Gary gave me a kind of fatherly smile. "Don't mention it. I know what it's like to have a Dad who isn't around. It's a different kind of hell most folks can't understand. If you need anything, you come ask for me. Toothpaste, anything."

The front doors slid open. Liz shuffled inside with her duffle bag slung over one arm. She looked paler than ever. I rushed to her side, but she wouldn't let me take her bag from her.

"You the older sister I heard so much about?" Gary said.

"Yeah," she said. "She's with me. Thanks for putting us up."

"It's no trouble." Gary looked from Liz to me and lifted his chin in thought. He knew we were lying, just not about what.

"Our apartment flooded," I said, side-eying Liz. "They have to clean our place, like I said."

"You didn't even have to tell him that." She glared at Gary. "I'm not a minor, which means I'm old enough to check into a hotel room without people poking their noses into places they don't belong."

"Whoa, hey, slow down." He raised his hands. "You girls just seem like you're in some kind of... situation. Just trying to help, is all."

"Thanks," Liz said. "But we don't need charity."

She turned on her heel and headed for the elevator as Gary shuffled away into his back office. I grabbed my bag and followed Liz inside the elevator. As the doors closed, I felt so bad about the way she had snapped at Gary. He was just trying to help, and she had been defensive in return. As I wrestled with how to manage my sister's mood taking a sudden downward spiral, Liz crossed her arms and leaned against the wall in a huff.

"That guy was so nosy," she said, rubbing her temples.

"He was just trying to help." I shrugged. "Besides, I kind of liked him."

She smirked. "You like everyone. That's the trouble. What if that guy was a creep? Two girls check into a hotel all alone. He might find a way up to our room with a spare key, and then we'd really be in trouble."

I couldn't argue that. She had a point, as much as I hated to admit it. I pushed the elevator button for our floor, and up we went.

"Are you okay?" I said.

She rubbed the bridge of her nose, a bad sign that one of her legendary migraines was riding the coattails of her bad mood. "I feel like death and that guy poking around our business got to me. The last thing we need is real life horror creeping into our already gigantic problems."

The elevator doors opened. We lugged our bags out into the hall.

"It's 316," I said, handing one of the room keys to Liz.

She lumbered down the hall, hissing air in through gritted teeth like it was all she could do to make it through the pain. It *was* one of her migraines, which explains why she had to take a second in the car and why she was in such a foul mood. I slid my card in the door, and the second it opened, Liz dropped her duffle to the floor and stumbled over to the bed in order to face plant into her pillow.

"Tylenol," she gasped.

She'd had bad migraines since she was fifteen, and every time she got one, it always completely took her out. I only remembered when they started because she got a really bad one at her birthday party and everyone had to go home halfway through. I wasn't really sure what the trigger was, but every time she had a bad episode, she had to sleep it off. I dropped my bag onto the bed by the window and returned to the duffle she'd discarded on the floor by the door. I rifled around until my hand hit a small bottle. Opening the bag up more, I found a first aid kit, two ice packs, and a rainbow of medicine bottles. I also found the red inhaler, the one I'd left back at the apartment. I smiled. *Operation Preparation Liz strikes again.*

I brought the Tylenol and a glass of water to her, but she told me to leave them on the night stand. I did what I was told and let her be, returning to the medicine stash to take my prescription. As I took in a big lung-full of the inhaler I got a huge whiff of the vanilla-scented room. Everything in here was as quaint and expensive looking as the decorations downstairs. This place wasn't a national chain, which meant someone who worked here was super into interior design. Someone put fresh flowers on the table and gold framed art with a sailboat on the wall. It was like stepping back in time, kind of like Gary's entire vibe.

I hopped up on the white and blue pinstriped comforter and let myself sink into the plush bedsheets. As my mind drifted, Liz let out a light snore. When I was sure she was asleep, I turned on the little TV, but my brain couldn't focus. My thoughts kept drifting back to Dad's journal and the gold markings on my arms. Marcus could see them. Why could he see them when no one else could? He might be a demon hunter, but he was just a guy. No special powers there.

I reached inside my duffle bag and pulled out the heavy leather book. The beginning entries detailed Mom and Dad's meeting under the study of Arturo to their perilous escape. I flipped through the entries where they struggled to keep the ghosts away from her while they searched for a way to stop the Sparrow curse entirely. Along the way, they found Banshees, Poltergeists, Wraiths, and Ghouls. There were pages of demons made entirely of eyes, aptly named "the Eyes." There was something called the Howler, a disgusting creature called the Plague, and a vague demon that was the worst of all—They called it "the Beast." There were places called "Haints," areas in the deep south known as Hollers, haunted ships at sea, villages of ghosts buried underwater, and great plains filled with the ghosts of Black Riders. I flipped to the back of the book where the pages stuck together and had to crack them apart to open them. My stomach gave a cold flop.

It's ruined. The last few journal entries are ruined.

The water must have seeped in more than I thought. All of Dad's handwriting was smudged. I sat on the edge of my bed while Liz snored, unsure of what to do. Some of his answers were completely gone. We'd have to figure out a huge chunk of information on our own. I flopped back on the pillow. The weight of the journal pressed on my chest as I breathed, reminding me too much of the Wraith. I pushed the book off me. The comforter was so soft I wrapped it around my body like a burrito. As my body relaxed, the categories shuffled through my mind like a deck of collectible cards. Dad and Mom must have fought them all. There was a record of each ghost, every demon, and all their statistics.

My eyes opened. *Demons have a weakness*— wards, sigils, the dark alphabet. I flipped to a page in the back of the journal. There was a smudge of what looked like letters. Infernal architecture. That's what the Poltergeist had called the dark alphabet. My vision blurred as I stared at the smudges, trying to imagine what they really looked like as I drifted off to sleep.

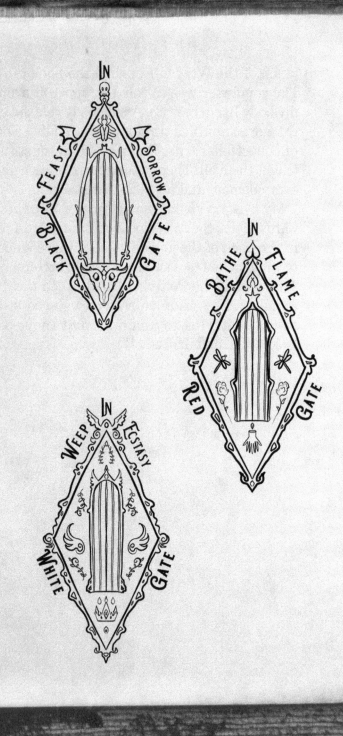

<u>Ghosts:</u> A spirit manifestation of that which was once human. Ties to house or place of death. Includes both spirits that were once human that refuse to move on, and spirits that re-enact personal hell as punishment. The latter is malevolent but responds to name used in life. Appears as human, astral light, or orb in shape.

Difficulty: Ranges from non-threatening to violent and threatening.

Warnings: Study from a distance. Engage only if not violent.

Weakness: Salt, iron, burning the bones, resolving past grievances, name.

<u>Demons:</u> Supernatural entities that were never human. Will do anything to ruin the lives of the living. Only goal is torment and to obtain a physical body. Other motivations remain unknown. When they obtain physical form, it is that of a monster. The best way to determine if an entity is a ghost or a demon is through the Sparrow of Summoning, though each resurgence will cost her in the form of equivalent exchange.

Warnings: Unstoppable, unrelenting. Avoid at all costs.

Weaknesses: Wards, sigils, the dark alphabet, demonic language.

<u>THE BEAST:</u> Image found in Arturo's journal. Everything else, unknown. (Emily is too afraid to recreate it.)

Warnings: DO NOT SUMMON

Weaknesses: Unknown

10

Kindling

LIZ'S PHONE BUZZED WITH her alarm. It trilled a little jingle, jarring me awake. I lifted my head off the pages of Dad's journal. At some point, I had rolled over and tried to become one with the Banshee page by using my own drool as adhesive. I wiped away the spit. Thankfully, it didn't smudge anything too badly, but I had smeared the hollow space where her mouth should have been. Thank God for small favors—I hated looking at her open throat.

I propped myself up to my elbows and turned to Liz, who was still not snoozing her stupid phone. It jingled again as she snored.

"Liz!" I took a pillow and threw it at her head. "Turn off your damn phone."

The pillow hit her square in the face. She grunted. "Huh? What?"

"Your alarm is so loud it's going to wake every dead soul in Savannah. Please, for the love of God, *turn it off*." I threw another one and this time it hit her in the stomach.

"Stop!" She groaned as she rolled over and formed a burrito with her sheets. "Just a few more hours."

"Whatever. You're the one who made a big deal about missing class, not me."

"I always set an alarm for two hours before." Her voice was muffled beneath the pillows. "There's time."

"You could have told me that," I groaned and flopped back on the bed.

Everything came rushing back—the symbols, the dark alphabet, the pages of demons and ghosts on display like some horrible zodiac. My eyes opened and I threw off the sheets. I swung my legs over the side of the bed, grabbed the journal, and pulled the pillow off Liz's head. "I found something last night."

She rolled over to look at me. The color had returned to her cheeks and her eyes were clear—a good sign her migraine was gone. "What is it? Can it wait?"

"No," I said, handing her the journal. "Not if you want to be completely unprepared the next time a demon attacks. This is Dad's journal, the one I told you about. He didn't just write about the Sparrow powers; he catalogued every demon they ever fought. There are sigils and some kind of dark alphabet. I think if we study them, we can protect ourselves until we find Dad."

"What are you talking about?" She sat up to take the book from me. "Dad fought demons?"

I took a deep breath. "We didn't know, but Dad was a ghost hunter. He took a record of his life. He wrote the entries, and Mom drew the pictures. They found a bunch of unusual ways to protect themselves but nothing that permanently got rid of the curse. Maybe that's what the obsidian necklace does."

"A ghost hunter?" She forced a laugh. "But Dad is so..."

"I know," I said. "He's all about vintage books and historical research and...not at all what I pictured a tough, battle-scarred ghost hunter to be. There was never any hint of the fact he came from some prestigious line of hunters. I never knew, did you?"

She shook her head as she cracked open the book. "No...but this does explain all of his less than pleasant quirks, like keeping ten bags of salt in the house. Once he painted these rocks with weird symbols and left them around the yard. I never could figure out why he did that."

"Me neither," I said. "But that's not all. Apparently, he studied under another family, led by this guy named Arturo. Here's where it gets really weird. Arturo kept mom prisoner at his house. Arturo was convinced Mom and her sister Amelia could combine their Sparrow powers to open some sort of door called the Black Gate. When Dad found out, he sprang them loose, but both Amelia and Arturo died in the process."

"That's horrible," she said. "

"And there's another thing." I flipped to the page I needed. "This family, I think they're here, in Savannah. I think that's where Dad went. I've been wondering if maybe Marcus is related to Arturo and Miriam. His family is into the occult, and from the way he fought the Wraith, he's definitely a ghost hunter too. He knew who the Sparrows were and about my mark."

"I can see why you want to find Marcus then." She stared at the picture of Mom and Amelia for a long moment. "Do you mind if I read it?"

"Be my guest," I said and handed her the journal. "The thing that gets me is at the very end of the entry, Dad says Arturo made Mom and Amelia conduct some sort of test to create a Mirror Door. I have no idea what it is, but it leads to this place called the Other, the same place I'm being pulled into. Apparently, this mirror can summon, but I don't think it means summon like I do—not give a ghost a body. Maybe that's how the demons found us. Maybe Miriam wants to lure us out of hiding to complete Arturo's work."

"Maybe." She rolled the sheets off and made herself more comfortable against the pillows with the journal. "We don't know anything for sure though and I feel super lost on all of this. I'd rather just read it for myself. Why don't you grab a shower? I'll read while you get ready and then we can head down for breakfast. I don't know about you, but I'm starving."

I did what I was told and headed inside the bathroom. I sighed as I turned the shower on and stepped in. The heat was more powerful than in Liz's apartment, even the smell was less salty. I relaxed into the routine of doing a basic clean instead of a scrub-blood-off-your-body one. Despite how relaxing the water felt, my mind wouldn't stop racing. My gut told me I'd stumbled into something big about my family that I could barely comprehend, but a huge question remained: did Miriam send the demons? Was she here in Savannah? Dad mentioned Arturo's wife took his death pretty hard—Was it enough to send demons after us? She was still out there. It took two Sparrows to create the Mirror Door, but did that mean Liz and I were next to open the Black Gate? Maybe that's why Mom hid away in our house all this time.

I dried off quickly and came out into the room wearing my towel, still wrestling with the impossible questions I had no idea how to answer. "So, how far did you get?"

Liz sat cross-legged on her bed, my favorite black hoodie in one hand, a white sharpie in the other. I nearly dropped my towel.

"What the hell are you doing?" I readjusted

before storming over to her. "That's my favorite! You're ruining it!"

She capped the pen. "Finished. I always was good at speed reading. It wasn't exactly War and Peace." She held it up and stretched my hoodie taut like a flag on proud display. "It's a ward. Dad drew a few of them in the book. What better way to protect ourselves than to use them? He said they could go on articles of clothing or be painted on rocks, which, again, explains the rocks he placed on the border of our property. This one is for protection. It actually looks kind of rad."

I took my hoodie back and rubbed my thumb against the circle and triangle connected by random letters. Much as I hated to admit it, the design did look pretty cool, like secret symbology made for an underground band. *Marcus. That's who it really reminds me of.* The symbol was just like one of the patches on his jean jacket. The letters were "A," "B," "A," and "S."

Liz showed me her gray running pull-over with the same symbol painted on the front. "See? We match. It won't be so bad, and at least it will protect us."

I took the journal and flipped to a deeper page in the book, one where there were upside down triangles. "As Above, So Below," I muttered.

"What was that?" she said as she pulled her shirt over her head.

I lay my hoodie on the bed. "I think that's what the protection symbol means. As Above, So Below."

She frowned at her pull-over. "That's sort of the essence of our power, isn't it? Banishment. Summoning. Maybe they're some sort of cosmic balance."

A feeling of recognition fluttered in my belly. Water dripped from my hair onto my shoulders and I shuddered. I forgot I was still wearing a towel. I went over to my duffle bag to fetch some clothes, turning over what she said in my mind. "You know, you seem to be taking this all better than I thought. I half expected you to be crying, or at the very least upset, when I came out of the shower."

She sighed. "You're not wrong. I *am* mad—I'm angry at Dad, I'm mad at you for not telling me— even though you tried to explain at breakfast. The thing is…when I saw you in the hospital, I realized something. Before Mom, you and I were close. I used to be there for you. You used to feel like you could tell me anything. So, I guess who I'm really mad at is myself. I almost lost you, and you didn't feel like you could tell me anything."

"But this isn't your fault," I said.

She wiped a tear from her cheek. "I know it isn't, but to be honest, I came here because I wanted to get as far from that empty house as possible. It just wasn't the same after Mom died. *I* was never the same. When we got back from the hospital yesterday, you could have told me about Dad, Mom, and everything else. Instead, you hesitated."

"I wanted to tell you," I said, tugged at the zipper on my hoodie. "I swear I did. I wanted to keep you safe, but I put you in danger with my silence. I'm sorry."

"You didn't want to, and *Dad* told you to keep me out of it." Her voice rose, but she paused and collected herself before continuing. "What I'm trying to say is because I shut you out, I'd made you feel like you couldn't tell me when things got *really* bad. If we'd talked last night, I could have put up wards in the apartment and then you wouldn't have gotten possessed."

"I've never felt so helpless." She cupped a hand over her mouth as her shoulders shook. I put my arm around her and waited for her to be able to speak again. "Seeing you possessed was the most horrifying thing I've ever seen. I never want that to happen again."

"I'm sorry." I shook my head to keep from crying, but it didn't last. I tried to wipe away the little tear circles on my white towel. "I felt guilty before, but I didn't know the whole reason of why Dad left me here. The way he managed it wasn't fair. Still, I'm sorry I didn't handle it better. I promise I'll tell you everything from now on."

"I will too." Liz opened her arms and I fell into them. "Don't worry. We'll find Dad, we'll figure out the curse, and I promise we will find a way to stop these demons."

She held me tight. As I buried my face in her pull-over, I closed my eyes and released all of the guilt I had been holding inside of me. I sighed, allowing myself for the first time that we really could banish this curse together.

Liz's phone beeped a shrill alarm.

"*Damnit*," she said. "My class is in thirty minutes. We have to go. Grab your things. We're out of here in five. We'll grab something to eat on the way."

"Um, it's the afternoon," I said as I took my clothes and headed into the bathroom to change. "I'm pretty sure they're done serving complimentary breakfast by now."

"They always leave the bagels," Liz said, her voice muffled by the bathroom door.

"And I can't believe you still want to go to class," I called back to her.

"I have a portfolio to turn in. We're going to Jen Library."

"Where is that?" I emerged wearing my blue jeans, black Halsey tee shirt, and my freshly marked black hoodie. At least with all this black, if I got blood on me later, the color would mask it pretty well.

"Down the street." Liz finished tying the laces on her shoes. "I had to complete some design research for Art History. It's super terrible. You have to cite at least twenty sources."

I raised my eyebrows as I packed Dad's journal into my bag.

"I know. It's ridiculous." Liz stuffed her art supplies and laptop into her duffle bag, leaving her clothing strewn across her bed. "But don't worry. You can hang out nearby and study Dad's journal. That symbol I drew should protect you."

She glanced at the baseball bat on the bed, reached for it and hesitated.

"Thanks for the jacket." I griped the inside of my hoodie sleeves tight. "I wasn't sure about it at first, but I really think it's going to work."

"Thanks." She forced a smile as she stuffed the bat into her duffle bag. "I have promising ideas some—" Her eyes widened, and her happy expression vanished. "Did you hear that?"

My breath caught in my chest. I was always the one who asked that question, not the other way around. "What did you hear?"

She shivered as she hiked up her duffle bag on her shoulder. "Children laughing. Can you not hear that, the scraping like tiny fingernails on the other side of the door?"

I shook my head, so she approached the door. She made her shoes as quiet across the carpet as possible. I followed her, but Liz gestured for me to stay back. I swatted her hand away. She wasn't going after some strange, unknown noise by herself. The air conditioning unit whirred to life behind me. A couple chattered down the hall on their way to the elevator.

Liz turned back to me, pale as morning frost on a windowpane. "They want to talk to us."

"What?" I said.

"The girls at the door."

"Well, don't open it!"

There was a knock, followed by a giggle and a scampering of feet across soft carpet. Liz reached into her duffle bag and pulled out her bat. She lay the bag gently on the floor, gripped the bat in one hand, and opened the door. She leapt out into the hallway.

I gripped the strap of my bag tight, waiting for her to return. When she came back inside and shut the door behind her, she gripped the bat so tightly I thought she might actually break the wood in half.

"There was no one out in the hall." The bat shook as much as her voice did. "I *know* I heard someone."

My skin pricked and a little wink of lightning played around my thumb. "We should get out of here."

"Agreed." She tucked the bat back inside her duffle and her eyebrows knit together as she examined my hand. "Does your power always do that?"

"Yes. When there are ghosts around."

Liz and I hurried down the hall towards the elevator. I'd never seen my sister walk so fast in my entire life. She pushed the down button way too many times. I had to grab her hand to get her to stop.

"It's going to be okay," I said.

"I'm fine." She stopped pressing and took a deep breath in. "Why did it have to be little girls?

They're so creepy."

I didn't know if she was saying that more to herself or me. She had a habit of talking to herself to solve problems. "I think you've seen *The Shining* one too many times."

The elevator came up one, two, three floors. The little bell dinged, and the doors parted. Someone was in the elevator already. Only it wasn't an alive someone.

In the South, we learned about the great war— aka the Civil War, aka the stupidly named "War of Northern Aggression." They slammed the information in our heads from elementary school all the way up to high school. It was hammered home so much I could remember every detail from the battles to the guns people used to what the soldiers wore. So, I knew the uniform when I saw it. I knew the brass buttons and gray fabric and the little hat. I'd never seen them on a ghost before, much less one with holes blown through its center and half of his face missing.

Bandages hung off the ghost's face as he leaned on a crutch. The Confederate soldier used his one, good, milky-white eye to find us as he reached for me.

"Sparrows," he said in a voice like rocks scraping on metal. ***"Let me see my darling Anna again. Give me a body. Please. I want another chance."***

"Should we banish him?" I said to Liz, but she wasn't standing beside me anymore.

Her bag swung against her back as she made for the stairs. I ran after her, a strange and unexpected smile pulling at the corners of my mouth. She might have taken care of one demon, but she wasn't used to this at all yet. Despite how much she loved horror movies, she was always the one who jumped. A little butterfly fluttered around in my stomach as I realized I wasn't afraid of this situation—my heart felt *light*. I checked up the stairwell to see if the soldier pursued us. He was hobbling along on his crutch as bits of his intestines jiggled out from the half-stitched slash in his stomach. He'd obviously died in the middle of some kind of surgery to his abdomen. I could give him life. I could touch him and make him whole again, but he would be a soul trapped out of time. No. He needed to stay buried in the past.

Liz reached the foot of the stairs and disappeared outside before I reached the lobby. Gary blinked at me as he sat behind the desk, his newspaper folded over from where he had stopped reading to watch my sister rush by. He pointed to the front double doors.

"Thanks," I said. "And this place wouldn't happen to be haunted would it?"

"Well," Gary said, twirling the curl of his mustache with a prim little smile. "It was a hospital for soldiers during the war. They turned it into a hotel. We've had a number of sightings reported. We're quite proud of the haunted happenings around here."

"Oh," I said. "Well, it would have helped to tell us that when we checked in."

"I'm sorry." He put the newspaper down. "Did you see something upstairs? You know we do love a good ghost story..."

I ran outside as fast as I could. I didn't have time to fill him in on the ghosts wandering his hotel. *Great. Just great.* Was there nowhere in this whole godforsaken city we could hide without ghosts emerging from every nook and cranny? As I left the Marshall House and found Liz's car still parked on the curb, I clenched my fists. She didn't drive away.

I checked both sides of the sidewalk and found her messy bun in the crowds of people heading about to cross the road. As I raced to catch up to her, my bag hit my sides with every step. Dad's journal struck my back over and over again with the weight of all the years, the lies, and the secrets my parents kept. I let out a mocking laugh.

We're never going to have a moment of rest, are we?

Protection Stones

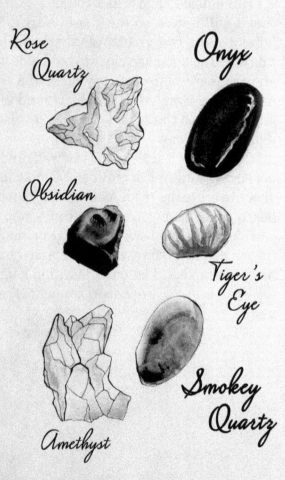

Rose
Quartz

Onyx

Obsidian

Tiger's
Eye

Amethyst

Smokey
Quartz

Emily and I found a way to block the spirits. I'd documented a series of symbols in an earlier entry. The symbol of protection seems to hold them off, at least for a while. We painted the outside of the van last night with it and we haven't heard anything for hours. Emily tries to sleep, but she keeps having nightmares. I don't remember the last time I slept a full night.

We need something more permanent. I can't drive another day. We need a place to land. We tried the wards in the hotel room, and they aren't able to get in. It's progress. Some progress. Emily made another crystal necklace with a pink stone she found in a gas station gift shop. I didn't think it was going to work, but Emily insists Rose quartz will help her heart heal and she'll be better able to use her powers. It's not the Obsidian necklace, but it's something.

Jacob
April 2, 1991

11

Library

LIZ WAS ALREADY HALFWAY across the street by the time I reached her. She had always been faster than me, having played softball and run track back in high school. Still, she had never just ditched me before.

"Hey!" I called after her. "Slow down!"

When she finished crossing, she wheeled on me and took me by the wrist. Her cheeks flushed as she pulled me to her and whispered into my hair. "Was that what I thought it was?" She had to ask me between breaths she was panting so hard.

"Yes. He was a ghost," I said, also trying to catch my breath. "Human shape means ghost. The hotel was a hospital during the Civil War."

She let me go. "Goddamnit."

"I don't think there is anywhere we can go. Not until we find a way to stop the curse or close the Mirror Door."

"The door?" she said. "Just because Dad's journal said Mom made a Mirror Door to the Other doesn't mean that's how the ghosts and demons are finding us. We have no idea what the Other is or what it does. Dad conveniently left those details out. Maybe you can do some research while I'm in class and find this Marcus guy?"

"They have a shop here," I nodded. "I can find the address when you're in class. Then we can form a plan to confront Marcus and find Dad. It would be nice to form a plan of attack instead of constantly acting on the defense."

"When we get to the library," she turned and started walking again. "I'm going to drop you in the lobby."

"Sure," I said as I jogged beside her. "Where exactly is SCAD anyway?"

She gestured to everything around us. "You're looking at it."

I shrugged. "That is a cafe, we just passed a clothing shop, and that is a movie theater up ahead."

"SCAD is laid out over several blocks," she said. "Admissions sits on one street, classes on another, and housing is just scattered. It took all of my first year to get used to which parts are Savannah and which are SCAD. On the older buildings, you can't tell them apart unless you read the signs."

She said nothing else as we ducked through the crowds of people and dodged slow-moving cars shoving their way through the pedestrians. My breakfast threatened to make a return appearance as I struggled to keep up. My jacket was uncomfortable to wear in the heat, but at least it protected me, and it hid most of the mark. I didn't want to look at it any more than I had to. A dull pain pulsed in my neck and shoulder from tossing and turning all night. Liz didn't look like she slept well either. She had put on makeup, but the dark circles remained.

"If the ghosts find us again, and you can't find me in Jen, meet me on the corner outside." She pointed to a white building across the road. "We're here. That's Jen Library."

Everything about Jen screamed modern. The enormous, square blue windows ran along the white slab that severed as SCAD's library. The logo was fashioned out of floating letters over the doorway. The pale building sat comfortably wedged between several brick buildings made entirely with Georgia brick, a distinct red clay that fades pink after weathering years of rain.

Students carried canvas bags, easels, stacks of books, and tote bags as they rushed in and out the sliding doors. Everyone was dressed like my sister, and they all seemed just as tired. Their hair came in every shade of dye and they wore clothes made from every hue of fabric. I adjusted the strap on my shoulder to better manage the weight of the duffle bag and waited for a space to open up in the crowd. I found an opening and ducked inside, happy to be lost among students again. For a moment I felt almost normal, until a blast of air conditioning hit me full in the face as soon as I walked through the doors. The sudden temperature difference made me stagger into another student. Even after all these years, I still wasn't used to the way every store from Atlanta to Savannah blasted air conditioning to combat the heat. You could be sweating one minute and freezing the next.

I sat down on a nearby bench and steadied myself, waiting for my body to adjust to the frigid indoor climate. Jen Library was just as modern inside as it was out. Chrome metal grates concealed long strips of fluorescent light high above me. Metal staircases fashioned out of wire, mesh, and pipes were so thin they seemed impossible to climb without falling apart. Two boys sat in gourd-shaped woven baskets that dangled from the ceiling. Students lounged on organic woodcuts molded together in spirals to form chairs. A trio of girls sat on green apples the size of Great Danes. It wasn't a library; it was a playground—an experiment in architecture and interior design. How did anyone focus on reading when there was so much to look at? Liz turned back, realizing she had lost me, and came to sit beside me on the bench.

"Don't worry," Liz said. "The protection spell

will work. I'll be back in an hour. Let's meet right back here at five. You'll be okay."

"You're right. I'll be fine," I said, but that was a lie. That little voice in the pit of my stomach wasn't feeling good about this at all. I didn't want to leave her, not when so much could happen without her. My sister smiled, waved, and left me alone on the bench. I watched her disappear into the stacks of Jen Library without me. The gold mark glittered in the corner of my eye. I shoved my hands in my pockets and dug my nails into my palms until I couldn't stand the pain anymore.

I was being ridiculous. I was prepared to go it alone from the beginning, and I could manage on my own for an hour or two while she was in class. Besides, with all these people here in such a modern-looking building, what was the worst that could happen?

I left the bench and climbed the loud stairs to the second floor. Every library is basically laid out the same—Fiction, Non-Fiction, Children's, Teens—but Jen Library was a completely different animal. As I navigated the aisles, I shook my head. There was no way we would find anything on ghosts here. The focus in Jen was on art reference and art history, from picture books to coffee table behemoths. Not the supernatural or anything remotely surrounding the occult.

I set my bag down on the floor next to an open computer. As soon as I clicked the mouse, it requested a student or guest login, which I didn't have. I groaned and abandoned the computer to find a place to hook up my laptop. I headed deeper into the aisles, happy to disappear between the stacks. There were a few tables open by the back windows, so I slid into an open seat and popped open my laptop. I tried logging into the Wi-Fi, but that required a password too. *Damn.* I slammed my laptop shut. So much for finding Marcus. I'd have to wait for Liz.

A boy with blue glasses whispered to a girl with pink and green bangs. I pull Dad's journal out of my bag and ignored them. I had bigger problems to worry about than what some college students thought of me. They kept talking and I glanced up to see if they were still talking about me, but they weren't. They watched a girl with a long tassel of black hair. It swished around her waist as she marched back to a nearby table with a stack of books. *Ashley?* Her back was to me as she placed a huge stack on the table and slid into her seat. She scribbled something into a notebook so quickly and angrily I couldn't follow her pen.

I left my things, approached her table, and tapped her shoulder. "Ashley?"

She gasped and turned around, a hand over her heart. They were wrapped to the point of mummification. Bandages covered her forehead and part of her jaw. Her ponytail revealed a bandage on her neck and collarbone. I guess they took the most hits from the glass shards. She didn't look even remotely like the confident, lovely girl I sat next to in science class. She was an exhausted, broken shadow of her former self. *I can't believe I'm the one who destroyed someone so beautiful. Marcus was right. This was all my fault.*

When she recognized me, she clasped a hand over her heart. "Jennifer. You scared me."

"Sorry. I didn't mean to," I said. "What are you doing here?"

I gritted my teeth as I saw her stack of books. *Haunted Savannah. Savannah: A Haunted History. Ghosts of Georgia. The Nature of the Demonic. Savannah's Occult Past and Present.* I swallowed hard.

"Are you okay?" She pulled the chair out next to her, indicating I should sit down. "The last time I saw you, there was this creature, and it was attacking you. I didn't know what happened after that. I'm so glad you're here. I could use your help."

"I'm fine," I said. "More or less. I have to use an inhaler…"

With a finger, she beckoned me to lean in, eyes wide and wild. "That thing, that *whatever it was*, it destroyed half the school. It wasn't an electrical fire or anything else they're claiming. I tried calling the newspaper to tell them, but they don't believe me. There was an actual ghost in our school, and it killed over half the students in our class."

Over half the students. So hardly anyone survived. What am I going to tell her? The truth

*is obviously off the menu. If she finds out what
really happened, and how I am the cause of all
of those students dying, she will try and turn me
in to the police.*

She shoved a stack of papers she'd printed off at me. "You'd think they'd admit something supernatural was going on. Savannah loves to boast about its ghosts, but not when it matters. Not only are they covering up what actually happened, but the fires won't go out. They keep dousing them with water, but they won't smother. Not entirely. I think there's something still there."

My stomach backflipped into my throat. *Is the Wraith still alive?*

She peered over her shoulder to check if anyone was listening. Two college girls with brightly dyed hair turned away from us and pretended to skim the titles in the Art History section. Ashley shot them a glare, and they scampered off.

"You believe me, right?" she said.

"Of course," I said. "We saw that monster. A lot of people did, but none of the witnesses are going to admit to the truth. It's one thing to believe in Savannah's history of the supernatural theoretically, another to outright admit a ghost tore apart our classroom."

She sighed. "You're right. I just didn't want to go through the struggle of convincing one more person to believe me. Mom doesn't. But there are half a dozen students still missing after the incident. No one is doing anything, so I'm going to."

This conversation was going super terrible. How could Ashley take on a creature like the Wraith? She'd be dead in five minutes. It was a miracle she was still alive at all. I had to come clean and tell her.

"Listen," I said. "That wasn't a ghost in the classroom…"

But Ashley didn't hear me. She was still going on. "Becky is one of the missing students. She's my best friend. I can't just…do nothing." She slammed her notebook shut and buried her face in her hands. "I can't lose my friend."

I bit down on my lip in an effort to keep myself from crying. Something *was* happening back at Northwinds. Maybe I didn't fully kill the Wraith. I didn't fully kill the Poltergeist. Liz did. Maybe Liz was the only one who could. Either way, I had to help her find Becky.

"I'll do it," I said. "I'll help you."

Ashley lifted her head. Her eyes were so red. "Really? Thank you. I'm so grateful you're here. It's so nice to have someone on my side. You and Marcus."

My heart twisted at the mention of his name. "Marcus? He's here?"

"That's right," Ashley said quietly. "You're new. You don't know. He and his family are ghost hunters. His grandmother runs this antique business on the riverfront, but everyone in Savannah knows the truth. If you want to deal with the things around here you can't explain, you need a Blackwell. He's on his way now. We were going to meet to figure out how to save Becky."

"He's coming here." I laughed a little too hard, unsure if I felt annoyed or relieved. "Of course, he is."

"Don't worry about him." She waved a hand away, like the answer was obvious. "He's fine, by the way. Hardly a bruise or bump. I envy him." She pointed to her arms and the dozen bandages. "I had to have over seventy-five stitches to get all the glass out."

I grimaced. "That's awful. I'm so sorry."

She eyed me up and down. "You barely have a scratch on you. How did you manage that?"

I should tell her. I really should explain...but what exactly? I tucked my hair behind my ear. "Guess I was lucky."

"Sparrow." A cool voice drifted in from behind me. "Didn't expect to find you here."

12

The Plan

MARCUS LEANED ACROSS THE table, looking as infuriatingly arrogant as ever. "I'm glad to see you're okay."

An angry blush flooded my cheeks. "I'm fine. Thanks."

He was wearing that jean jacket with patches again. Ashley was right. There wasn't a scratch on him. He looked perfectly normal, healthy even. It was impossible. He had been tossed, beaten, pummeled, yet he was bright-eyed and well-rested. *What the actual hell?*

"How is your mark doing?" he said and tossed his hair out of his eyes. My nose wrinkled as I tried to image all the things I would throw at his thick head. He grinned at me when I didn't answer, and I rolled my eyes at him.

"What mark?" Ashley said, breaking the heated silence between him and me.

"Yes, Sparrow, what mark?" Marcus raised his eyebrows at me, expecting me to answer. *What a jerk.*

"It's nothing. Just got a cut from the ghost," I said and glared at him so hard I hoped his soul would burst into flames.

"Thanks for coming," Ashley said. "I brought Jennifer up to speed about Becky. I was hoping to convince her to come tonight."

"Tonight?" I asked. Marcus said the same thing at the same time.

"Yes," she continued, looking from Marcus to me with her brows knitted together in confusion. "Marcus and I are heading back to Northwinds tonight to find Becky. Do you want to come with us?"

I owed her after causing the Wraith to rampage through the school, but was it the smartest idea to invite a Sparrow on a ghost hunt? Especially one who could give supernatural beings a body if she came into close contact? Not really. But I had watched the Wraith burn away in the presence of the Protection symbol with my own two eyes. Marcus had slit its throat. There's no way the Wraith survived.

My eyes narrowed and Marcus glanced at me, a quick little acknowledgement there was something important he had buried down inside himself so deep, no one could pull it out. He had to be Arturo's grandson. I thought back to the titles of the articles I'd read that called his family "thieves," "liars," and "con artists" of the supernatural. They swindled people out of their money using ghosts, and it all had something to do with their antique shop. As he turned back to Ashley, my instincts sent up all kinds of red flags. He was using her for something, but what?

"I'm not sure that's such a good idea," I said.

"But why?" she said. "We need all the help we can get."

Marcus smirked. "You would do anything it took to find Becky, right?"

This smelled like a trap. I smirked at Marcus and he stared me down, expecting me to shrivel. I didn't back down, or break eye contact. "Can I talk to you? Alone?"

Ashley shrugged as I grabbed Marcus by the wrist and whisked him through the aisles. I didn't know where I was taking him, only that it was as far out of Ashley's earshot as possible. We stumbled across one of the private study rooms that were meant for one person maximum. I flung him towards the door. "In there."

"I'm not going in there with you," he laughed. "There's no room."

He rolled his eyes and did as I asked. I followed him inside the tiny closet space, but it was entirely too close for comfort.

"I need some answers," I said. "And I need them

now. Who are you? How do you know my family?"

"Keep it down," he hissed at me. "Do you want everyone on the damn planet to know who you are?"

"I'm not going to keep it down," I said. "You made it seem like you were surprised I was dumped in Savannah, but I think you knew about it from the beginning."

"I didn't know you were here," he said. "But you know what I do know? Brent was my friend, and he's dead because of you. Now there is a new entity and it took Becky. The last thing we need is you coming along and summoning again."

"Is it the Wraith?" I asked. "Didn't I kill it?"

"Of course you did." He groaned as if I could not stop spouting the world's stupidest questions. "It's not the Wraith. The ward always works whether it's ghosts or demons that need to be put down. I think it's something else, drawn by you. When you cross an entity over, it leaves a mark like a beacon. You just rang the dinner bell for every supernatural dying to cross over, and in Savannah, that's a hell of a lot. Let me take care of it. Leave this place."

The salt knife. Dad's journal mentioned a salt knife. He was trying to distract me from asking questions about his family.

"You're avoiding my question!"

"And you're going to get in the way." Marcus's voice rose. "You don't even have a handle on your powers yet!"

"Yes, I do." I crossed my arms. "I used my powers to burst a Poltergeist yesterday. I can explode whatever took Becky and my sister can banish it, but that's beside the point because—"

"The Sparrow of Banishment is awake?" His eyebrows raised. "What am I saying? Of course she is. When one wakes up, the other one must too. That's how the balance in the universe works. It doesn't tolerate the imbalance created by one of you existing alone. 'As Above So Below.' You are the 'below' half of that equation."

I blinked. "Okay, so I didn't know that."

He huffed at my comment, so I rolled my eyes. "*Whatever.* I don't care what you think of me. All I care about is why you know so damn much. How did you know I'm the Sparrow? How did you know about my family?"

"Because that's what my family does." His green eyes flashed. "We train demon hunters. That is all we do, all we talk about, from the time I wake up until I go to bed. I dream of spell work and wards. It's horrible. We know everything about the supernatural and we're supposed to protect people from it. My family exists to clean up your mess."

I stumbled back and brushed up against the little desk mounted into the wall. I'd come here to confront him, but I never considered that the villain might be me. We did create carnage wherever we went, and the Sparrows seemed to exist to only cause pain to the living.

"Why did you save me from the Wraith?" I said quietly.

He shook his head, taken aback by the question. "What?"

My voice trembled, but I had to say the horrible thing I was thinking. "If I am such a destructive force, why save me at all?"

He looked at me with so much pity it made me sick. "Because for all of your destruction, for all of your potential to destroy the lives around you, if you learned to harness your power, you could use it for good."

Dad's words coming from Marcus. *The potential for good?* Tears formed hot trails down my cheeks, but I lifted my chin. I didn't care. Let him see me cry. "That's the same stupid thing my dad said, and you know what? He abandoned me instead of helping me, just like you. You love to criticize, but never put yourself in my shoes. How would you feel if you had a terrible power that only killed everyone around you? How would you feel if one day you woke up and found you've lost control?"

I punched the wall before I realized what I had done. I grimaced when there came a loud bang back from the student in the neighboring study room, a passive-aggressive form of "shut up." I shook my hand out to get rid of the pain but one of my knuckles bled like stink.

"Let me take a look," he said, and retrieved a Band-Aid from one of his jean jacket pockets. He took my hand and inspected my knuckles. "It's hard to tell with all the gold, but you have a cut."

"Is the equivalent exchange going to take me?" I said in a soft voice. "Is there a cure?"

He placed the black bandage across my knuckles. My face flushed and I couldn't tell if it was from lingering anger or something else. His green eyes met mine as he finished sticking it on.

"I don't know," he said with a voice as smooth and deep as velvet. "I'm sorry."

"No cure?" My stomach turned to lead in my gut.

"If there is a way," he said, gripping my hand a little tighter, "I will help you find it. Maybe we can help you. We help a lot of people find their way. My grandmother, she trains ghost hunters. She runs a shop that deals in haunted antiques and rinses them clean again. She might be able to help you control your powers."

Something the Wraith said came back to me.

You weren't supposed to kill me.

She will have your head for this.

Miriam.

She was the one who sent the Wraith.

My original theory wasn't wrong.

"You're related to Arturo," I said, pulling my hand away. "Aren't you?"

For the first time since I met him, fear grew in Marcus's wide eyes. "He was my grandfather."

The entire world dropped out from under me. I was right. Arturo was Marcus's grandfather. Dad was here to find the Blackwell's. They had the Obsidian necklace. My eyes fell on the dark crystal around his neck.

"Is that...the Obsidian necklace?" I said.

"No." He clutched the crystal tight. "Why are you asking?"

A ticking sound went off in my head, a whirring like beetle wings. My legs wobbled at the sudden shift in pressure and I fell into the wall.

"Are you okay?" He reached out and steadied my shoulder. His hand was soft, warm.

Something buzzed nearby, like a bumblebee trapped behind a screen door. It hummed and whirred, ascending in volume until I had to cover my ears. My skin pricked as if the air units had kicked on again, but the room didn't have a vent.

"Can't you hear that?" I yelled to be heard over the buzzing.

"No!" he said, winching at the volume of my voice. "Why are you yelling?"

The window of the conference room burst outward. Pane after pane exploded, rippling from window to window like a wave on the ocean. I ducked against the wall, still clutching my ears. Marcus said something, but I couldn't tell what. My head rang with the pressure and high-pitched sound.

Little flakes of blue light sparked at my fingertips. *Damn. Not again.* I crawled out from under the table, taking care not to touch the glass.

"It's a ghost," I said. "Or a demon. It's here."

Marcus and I scrambled out of the little room back into the library. Someone ran into me, full-on. A girl smacked into my shoulder, and I caught the table with my hip. I limped through the current of students as they ran past me and screamed at each other to run. We raced back to our table and found only Ashley's books there.

"Ashley?" Marcus said, whirling around.

But there was no sign of her in the throngs of clamoring students. The humming returned and rose again to a painful pitch. I covered my ears and kept going, searching for any sign of her. A sensation stirred in the pit of my stomach, deep and familiar. My palms itched with pressure, the same as before. A pulse inside my body made my bones vibrate with a sharp pain. A trail of lightning, red this time, cracked up the backs of my marks. *Oh no.*

"She's over there," he said. "Come on."

I followed Marcus down the aisle, out into the center of the stacks. My heart pounded as I tried to figure out what the red lightning meant. The crowd parted to reveal Ashley floating in mid-air. Her shoes dangled over the metal stairs leading to the first floor. Her black hair billowed up all around her like she was floating underwater. Her mouth parted wider than should be possible. She screamed. The sound was excruciating and inhuman, but full of rage and grief, like she was lamenting the world for all its sorrows.

She's possessed.

Marcus and I covered our ears, but that wasn't enough to muffle the sound. He called out her name to break her out of it, but it was like throwing a dish rag at a house fire. Blood dripped from the corners of her eyes down both cheeks. She lifted a limp hand in front of her, as though her wrists were pulled by invisible strings. Her fingers stretched, and a boy went sailing past me in a blur of blue hair. He punched and kicked the air, but he couldn't escape whatever force lifted him to her.

"Ashley, let him go!" Marcus said.

She wrapped the student in her embrace and grinned as she squeezed the screaming blue-haired boy.

"No." Her voice was soft as a lullaby. *"You shall not have my child."*

The voice was rich, feminine, and almost melodic. It was the voice of a mother, the voice of a kiss good night, of a warm "I love you."

"I know your name," he said. "I'm begging you, Banshee. Release Ashley. She's not worth possessing to get to the Sparrow."

It wasn't a demon. It was a ghost. I remember that page from Dad's journal. They only wanted one thing—to take whoever they viewed as their children. They were the more powerful of the ghosts because of the ferocity of their mourning. The Banshee inside Ashley cooed against the blue-haired boy's ear. She squeezed tighter as the poor student begged her to let him go.

"That isn't your child!" Marcus shouted.

Ashley looked down her nose at me. *"And she*

is not the Sparrow I want."

There was a sickening pop as his ribs broke. The wails silenced as the body went limp in her arms. She petted his hair, whispered sweet adorations in his dead ear.

Marcus hesitated and then reached in his pocket and pulled out his knife. He didn't look at me as he whispered, "Let me handle it."

"The Sparrow I want. She is here."

"Jennifer!" Liz was running up the stairs.

Ashley turned away from us, no longer interested in either of us or the boy. She dropped his body onto the steps with a sickening crumple and floated towards Liz. A ballet flat slipped off her dangling foot and clanged on the stairs below.

Liz drew her baseball bat up to her face. "Stay away from my sister."

The Banshee inside of Ashley laughed as if she'd just told an exceptionally fine joke. *"But I have no need for the Sparrow of Summoning. It's you I want."*

A knife sliced into Ashley's leg. I hadn't been watching Marcus. He'd followed Ashley and sliced his bone-white knife down her thigh, hard enough to draw blood. She howled and clawed at where the skin now hissed.

"What the hell are you doing?" I yelled. "Don't hurt her!"

"I'm not!" Marcus yelled back. "I'm trying to draw it out of her!"

Marcus yanked her down by the ankle, and

Ashley dropped, landing on top of him. Where she once hovered, an outline of a woman shimmered—a bit of sheer, opalescent fabric hanging in mid-air. The Banshee's long cotton dress trailed over her dripping feet. Her delicate form gave her the appearance of a doll fashioned out of tissue paper. And then I saw her face. The space below her nose was ripped off entirely, exposing her windpipe and pink vocal cords for all the world to see. Little bits of muscle hung loose from her jaw bone and cheeks, stretched thin like runny egg.

The Banshee screeched at Marcus, throwing him back. She swooped down and picked Liz up by the stomach. Liz dropped her bat as the Banshee soared out the open window and into the sunlight. Marcus pushed Ashley off him, reached for Liz, and missed her leg by a few inches.

Liz. The Banshee has Liz.

No. It couldn't take her. Not my sister.

Not Liz.

"Damn it," he said. "We don't have much time."

Ashley sat up, clutching her head. "What the heck just happened?"

Marcus turned to me. "We have to go after her. If we don't, it will force Liz to use her powers and more of her will be sucked over."

My breath caught in my throat. "What? But she doesn't have a mark. How is that possible?"

"Her feet," he said. "The Sparrow of Banishment always starts a mark on her feet."

"Hey," Ashley said. "What happened to my leg?"

"Sorry." Marcus retrieved a roll of bandages out of his jacket pocket and handed them to Ashley. "I didn't forget about you."

"You just carry bandages in your pockets all the time?" I said.

He side-eyed me. "When the Sparrows are awake, yes!"

He kneeled and helped Ashley bandage the long gash down her leg. "It stings," she said. "But I can walk. What happened?"

"You were possessed by a ghost, and it took Jennifer's sister," Marcus explained. "It's probably better if you stay here and wait for the emergency crews to arrive."

"No," she said. "I'm going with you. My leg is fine."

"I really don't think—" Marcus tried to say but Ashley cut him off.

"I didn't ask what you thought, I'm telling you. I'm going with you. Let's get Becky and Jennifer's sister back." She turned on her heel and started hobbling towards the front doors.

"So, what now?" I said. "How do we find where it went?"

"With this." He drew something out of his pocket, a black and gold flecked cut gem at the end of a long chain. He held it out in front of him, dangling it from one hand, until it steadied. The crystal quivered as it leaned away from him, pointing to the street outside. "It's a pendulum," he explained. "All we have to do is follow where it points, and it will lead us right to Liz and the Banshee."

13

The Other

THE PENDULUM SWAYED IN front of Marcus as he turned down another street. The sun was low in the sky, and the hanging moss covered most of the pink light of the setting sun. It would be dark in less than two hours. I hoped we could find Liz before nightfall. Ashley followed Marcus at a faster pace than I thought she'd be able to with her injury. I wasn't going much faster than her. My duffle bag swung back and forth as I struggled to keep up with his tall gait. I couldn't find Liz's bag, but I had stuffed Liz's bat into mine. It rested on top of Dad's journal, which meant I brought up the rear of our weird little parade through Savannah. I stopped only when I needed to catch my breath, which was about every ten feet. My cough had come back a bit since the library, but it could wait until I got back to the hotel. Finding Liz was more important than anything else.

Marcus stopped. Ashley ran into him.

"Why are you walking so fast?" she snapped. "And then stopping so much?"

"It won't work unless I'm still," he snapped back.

The little pendulum swayed between his fingers. It swirled around in little circles, so fast it was hard to keep track of the crystal on the end of the chain. It stopped. The tip pointed forward toward a strip of shops and restaurants. I knew this street. I remembered the little cafe and clothing boutique from my walk to school.

"It's definitely pointing at Northwinds," Marcus said. "Which aligns perfectly with the missing students."

"Do you think it has Becky?" Ashley asked.

"It tracks," he said. "The Banshee was likely looking for her child, and kept taking people, but no one was a suitable substitute. But I'm worried because this type of ghost tends to…" He paused, looking away from her like he didn't want to finish the thought. "It will dispose of anyone it doesn't want."

"Oh," she said and bit her lip to keep from crying, but it wasn't working.

The blue-haired boy. Did Ashley remember what she did when the Banshee was inside her? Or was she worried Becky might be dead? I remembered the entire incident of being possessed, but I wasn't sure if that was normal or just because I was the Sparrow. I didn't want to bring that up now. It would definitely upset her to hear she'd actually killed someone, and she didn't need to be reminded if she *did* remember.

"Do we use your knife to get rid of the Banshee, or should we use my symbol?" I said, changing the subject. "I have one on the back of my jacket. Would that burn it away?"

Marcus shook his head, but he smiled a little, clearly relieved I had hijacked the conversation. "Banshees are not demons, and they are extremely specific in what they want. It's a blanket term we use for the ghosts of mothers. They do tend to collect anyone they view as a child, but it makes them both easier to spot and harder to get rid of. The wards won't work the same way on ghosts like Banshees. They're very *single-minded,* but all we have to do is find its nest and use the salt knife to kill her."

Dad mentioned using a salt knife to kill Arturo. If that's the case, and Marcus carried the same weapon... that meant the knife glittering in his back pocket killed his grandfather. I grimaced. Marcus raised an eyebrow at me, but I just looked away. I didn't want to be the one to explain he was carrying around a murder weapon.

The pendulum shook as it pointed in the direction of Northwinds, turning his attention away from me. He sprinted down the road, forcing

Ashley and I to jog in order to catch up with him. We dodged past a romantic couple as they stumbled with two red cups full of brown liquid. I kept forgetting people were allowed to walk around the city with alcoholic beverages. Back home, you rarely saw people drink except at restaurants and festivals. It was so unusual to have such a lax rule this deep in the Bible-belt South, but that's Savannah for you.

We turned down another street I recognized. The golden dome of City Hall peeked over the trees. The setting sun reflected off its surface, casting the surrounding treetops in a warm glow. I breathed in the smell of saltwater rising up from the river, and my shoulders relaxed a little. A low purr of thunder crackled in the distance. I turned towards the east. Clouds billowed in from the direction of the sea. We needed to get to Northwinds before the sky opened up again.

Rage burned like a struck match inside my heart as my body roared with the need to release all my fury into the Banshee for taking my sister. I'd unleash everything into her until she shattered. Let my mark spread. I didn't care. I could figure out how to reverse it after I tore the Banshee apart.

Marcus turned the corner and skidded to a halt.

"What is it now?" Ashley said.

"Sorry," he said. "It's just...look."

He pointed down Bull Street towards Johnson Square. While the rest of the city sparkled with

167

bustling people, cars, and the blaring sun, the square and its surrounding buildings were completely dark, as if it were midnight but only on this one street. The hairs on the backs of my arms raised. There were no people. Not a single pedestrian, tourist, or even a dog walker. Everyone was walking around it, away from it, unconsciously avoiding the area. They passed by as though Bull Street wasn't even there.

"This is really bad," Marcus said.

"I don't like the sound of that," Ashley said.

"It's the Other." He pocketed his pendulum. "In places that become very haunted, a sort of veil spreads throughout the area. But the entity has to be really toxic to poison a place like this."

"The Other?" My ears perked. "What is that?"

"It's the realm between the living and the dead," he said. "Spirits get trapped there on their way to the other side because they can't break cycles that occurred when they were alive. It's usually because they have committed horrible crimes like violence and murder or because of major emotions like guilt and longing. They wander the Other trapped in their own personal hell."

An icy wave of fear ran from my spine down to my toes. I knew that already. Somehow, I *knew*.

"The living can't see the Other, can they?" I stepped aside to let a mother with a stroller by. "They're not even looking at it."

"No," said Marcus. "They're aware of it in a subconscious way. You know the shiver you get looking down a dark empty hallway, when you know something is there you can't see? That's the Other. That's why they're avoiding Northwinds. They know. They just can't put their finger on why."

Liz and I followed Marcus down the misty road, away from City Hall toward Johnson Square. It was so dark I had to pull my flashlight out of the duffle bag in order to see. It illuminated the road and the sidewalk but not much else. The rest was all fog.

"Maybe you should lead," Ashley offered. "You have the light."

Marcus pocketed the pendulum. "She's right. We know where the Banshee is now. Light the way, Sparrow."

"Okay," I said, not at all nervous, not at all still angry at Marcus.

I took the lead, lighting the way down Bull Street. The beginning of the road was mostly non-descript buildings and white walls. When we reached the fork, I turned right at the obelisk with lush foliage surrounding the monument in Johnson square. Our group took it slowly as we approached the front gate of Northwinds.

Yellow caution tape flickered around a thick chain that hung heavily and wrapped around the iron on the gate. Thick, gray fog blotted out the rest of the landscape and brick buildings. I peered between the shuttered ironwork. The windows did not reflect the light emanating from the nearby street lamps. Thick oak branches moaned as they collided with each other in a whistling wind. Marcus shook the gate to try and break in, but the chain only rattled.

"There must be another way in," I said.

He pointed to the cafe next door. "There's a back way if we go through the kitchen. We hop the wall and go in through the greenhouse at the back of the school."

"Well, no sense waiting," Ashley said, pushing past him. "Let's go."

A little bell chimed as she opened the door to the cafe. No one stood in the entranceway behind the podium. There were no servers or people waiting for tables. I touched the podium and found the list of reservations. The colors were all muted, even the highlighter that ran across the table names. I backed away. The saturation on the world had turned down halfway, painting everything into shades of gray.

Marcus and Ashley followed me through the foyer into the seating area. The tables were all laid out for dinner—flatware, napkins, half-full glasses, plates of steaming food—but nobody sat in the chairs. The restaurant was completely empty.

"Hello?" My words carried like lines delivered on stage to an empty theater and the sound of my voice fell flat. "Is anyone here?"

"So weird," Ashley said as she approached the bar area. There was a drink at every stool, but no one was there to drink them. In the back, a stage sat covered with instruments—a sax, trumpets, guitar, bass, and a full drum kit. Beyond the bar, a staircase led to an upper level with more seating.

"What the hell?" She picked up a glass of alcohol off the bar. A trickle of condensation ran down the side of the glass. Ice the size of golf balls clinked around inside the amber liquid. If the ice was still whole, the drink was fresh. Someone had just left it there only moments ago. She put down the glass and examined one of the knifes on the table, used the tip to poke a flank of steak. Steam rose off the muted pink center.

"It's like Dorothy," Ashley said. "Only, we're traveling back to Kansas from Oz. Where is the color?"

"Because it's the world but not quite the world," he said, running his hand along a table set for two. "Ghosts live in a world without taste, without feeling, without any kind of pleasure."

I could see why they wanted to escape, why the ghosts yearned for my power so badly. If I were stuck here, I'd give anything to get out. I glanced down at the mark and swallowed hard. Even in this dampened world, I shimmered. It wasn't just the marks on my arms, my whole body gave off a faint golden glow, like a candle in an empty room. *That's how they see me.* That's how they were always finding me no matter where I was.

"It's your power," Marcus said in my ear. "It's always coming off you. It's like I said, you're a beacon in the dark. Don't worry. Ashley can't see it."

I rolled my eyes. "I know. And don't think I've forgotten who you are, or what your family did to my mother."

He scratched the back of his head. "I don't know what you mean."

"Shouldn't we go?" Ashley said. "I thought we didn't have time to waste."

"Sure," I said, shoving past Marcus.

He smiled at me, amused. Seeing him smile was so very wrong, especially because up until this point, he'd been a colossal jerk. Plus, his grandfather held my mom hostage to use her powers for his personal gain. How could he not know that? Did his family not tell him? Just because we had to team up to save my sister didn't mean I had suddenly forgotten everything. I would just have to put the Blackwell problem on pause. After we saved Liz, I was getting answers about Dad and I didn't care if Marcus wanted to give them or not.

"I've never seen a spirit infection this invasive," he said, picking up a half-full wine glass and sloshing the gray liquid around. "Normally, the Other spreads from the haunted area that's been poisoned to just the boundaries of the house it haunts. This has taken over the whole street. The Banshee is going to be incredibly powerful."

"How are we going to get out of here?" Ashley said, setting the knife down.

He put the wine glass back where he found it. "Once we release the Banshee, the world will right itself. We can't stay too long, or it will be even harder to get out. The Other has a way of keeping things here, especially living things."

A voice whispered against my ear. I whipped around, shining my light in the direction of the sound.

"What is it?" Marcus said.

"Nothing yet," I said. "Thought I heard someone."

He nodded. "Let's keep moving."

Marcus bumped into tables and chairs as he navigated to the kitchen door, a pivoting metal thing that might as well have been made of tin. Ashley caught the door in the back swing and disappeared inside after him. I caught the metal door and followed the same pattern. Completing all of these steps silently was important—it felt best to not make noise or attract too much attention. A humming bee sound grew as we advanced into the kitchen. I whipped around; certain a strand of hair had been plucked off my head. There was nothing behind me, but I couldn't shape the feeling that something watched us. I hoped it was only the Banshee and nothing else.

We advanced through the kitchen as a group, keeping each other close. The path between shelves of pots and pans and the wall was so narrow we had to squeeze. Even Marcus's shoulders were tense as he took the lead, choosing his steps with care as we moved in single file against the wall. He kept turning around to check behind us, which put me on edge even more than I already was.

"Look," Ashley said. It was all she dared to say in the quiet.

I peered between the aluminum bowls on the high shelves that divide the kitchen in half. Water boiled on the stove, hissing as it overflowed onto the coils beneath. Oil popped in a cast-iron pan. Fillets of breaded chicken had turned a crisp golden brown. Dishes sat piled in a bubbling sink, the water pouring with no one to turn it off, but it never overflowed. The water didn't pour down. It flowed upward, drawing from the sink and back up into the faucet.

"What the hell is happening to the water?" I whispered.

"Everything works in reverse here," Marcus said. "Water, leaves, rocks: they all fall up instead of down. Only the living move forward."

He paused and drew a finger to his lips, a request for silence. We waited for a sight or sound, some movement.

There was a booming crash, a twinkling of shattered china. A bowl rolled across the floor and came to rest near the sink.

The kitchen door popped open, revealing a woman so thin her bones shone through her paper skin. Wisps of thin, gray hair billowed around her shoulders. Her body was sheer, paler than a cloud, and we could make out the outline of the restaurant through her ribcage. As she hovered, ink dripped from her toes to the ground beneath her bare feet. Ribbons of her exposed vocal cords vibrated like violin strings.

The Banshee had found us.

14

Northwinds

"RUN!" MARCUS YELLED, BUT it was too late. The Banshee opened her broken throat to sing and the world exploded. I was only aware of what happened to me, that my body went flying, that pots and pans pummeled me from every direction. Then the floor came up fast and gave me a big sucker punch kiss to the face.

I groaned. Everything everywhere hurt. I tried to figure out what was up and what was down and which direction my head was in, but the world still vibrated even though the Banshee had stopped screaming. I couldn't hear, couldn't see—It was like a bomb had blown up next to my head.

I threw a mixing bowl off and pushed up to my hands and knees. Ashley lay in front of me, sprawled out like a starfish. Her purple Converse shoes were falling off her feet. I grabbed her ankle and called out her name, but I couldn't hear myself. *The Banshee*. It had screamed so loudly I couldn't hear anything but a vague ringing. Ashley lifted her head and turned to say something, but I mouthed that I couldn't hear.

Marcus grabbed my wrist and yanked me up so hard I worried he'd pull my arm out of the socket. He stumbled across the kitchen, holding the side of his head as a thin stream of blood trickled down the bridge of his nose. Sweat beaded across his forehead as he gestured for us to get up, go, run. A small knife of panic twisted in my heart. There was no fighting the Banshee; there was only running from her. He must have never faced anything like the Banshee before.

I got to my feet and helped Ashley up, even though my legs shook. *I can do this. I can use my powers for good.* Marcus and Ashley took my lead as I ran toward the back door. Together, we tumbled across the pots, pans, and aluminum bowls out into the darkness of the alley.

My tennis shoes found a puddle and skidded across. I turned around, but the rain hammered so hard it was impossible to tell the shapes apart. I call out to Ashley and Marcus, but my voice came out muffled, like I was screaming into a pillow. They were gone, and I couldn't see the back of Northwinds at all. *My flashlight.* I searched my duffle bag, but there was only Dad's journal, some pens, and Liz's bat. I must have lost it back in the kitchen. I took a deep breath and let my eyes adjust. Red light blinked around my gold mark. *My mark.*

I peeled off the wet sleeves and tied the jacket around my waist in the hopes the protection symbol would still work. The gold mark shimmered bright enough to see the outlines of the restaurant building and the brick wall behind Northwinds. The shop's windows ran the length of the alley, and the glass didn't reflect my light. The windows of Northwinds were just as dark and empty, though I could swear I saw movement in the second floor. Footsteps fell on the puddles behind me and I whipped around.

Marcus took my hand in his. I held my other hand out into the rain, and in two breaths, Ashley's soft fingers touched mine. She smiled, blinking rain out of her eyes in order to see us. He nodded, motioning for us to follow him into the mist. We formed a chain, clinging to each other like we were back in elementary school and trying not to get lost. For the first time, I was glad he had offered his hand. It was comforting to be connected to both of them as the Other pressed our bodies together in the wet darkness.

Water fell both up and down, thundering on us from overhead and cycling back up from the puddles into the sky. The wall surrounding the garden behind Northwinds was bigger than I expected, and it was covered with ivy so dense

I couldn't make out the bricks. Marcus let go of me and reached up and found a ledge. He hoisted himself up carefully over the jagged ironwork fencing that ran along the top before turning around and motioning to follow his lead.

"You next," I whispered and gestured for Ashley to climb. She shook her head, clearly arguing I should go next, but we'd run out of time. I led her to the wall, but I didn't want to let go of her hand. Our eyes met. I never knew she had gray flecks in her brown eyes.

She was so close, and our hands lingered far longer than I knew what to do with. Her lips brushed mine with the swiftest kiss, so quick I didn't know if it happened. When she withdrew, I put a hand to my lips and watched her repeat Marcus's pattern. Heat flooded my cheeks as she mounted the wall with a push.

Had she really just...*kissed me*?

Ashley straddled the ironwork as she leaned over to check if I was okay. Marcus had already vanished behind the wall into the garden below. She beamed at me, biting her lip a little as she blushed, and it was the most adorable thing I had ever seen in my life. She really did kiss me.

A clang echoed across the alley and a trashcan lid rolled over to us like a tossed quarter. It hit the wall with a bang. *The Banshee*.

I shook my head, brought myself back to the moment, and gave her a thumbs up. A shadow passed behind her smiling face like a dark curtain.

Ashley must have seen my expression because she turned in time for the Banshee to open her throat. The scream blasted in her face and Ashley went tumbling off the wall.

I tried to catch her, but the Banshee turned her head and the sound hit me like a tidal wave. For a breath, all I saw were bricks and leaves, and then my shoulder hit the ground. Pain erupted as my right shoulder took the full impact of my fall. I tried to roll over, but it hurt too much to move. My vision swam in waves. It was hard. It was so, so hard to keep from blacking out. All I could do was blink up at the rain.

Ashley's shoes dangled over me. Her arms and legs hung limp by her sides as the Banshee carried her by her waist up into the second story window.

"Ashley..." I reached for her shoe, but it was too far away.

No.

I can't let this happen again.

I can't.

The power to do good.

A fire woke inside me.

Up until that moment, my Sparrow gift had slept in the center of my body, only emerging when I called. After the deed was done, it would retreat back into a dreamless sleep. The Sparrow power was a sensation I could feel every moment, like red butterflies fluttering around in my stomach. I had not brought it out fully, not really, not until my rage emerged like a fiery bird from the hollow of my former self. I had been naïve, so timid, and terrified to think I couldn't call on a part of me that was as natural as breathing.

Fire boiled my insides and raced through my veins like poison. The heat traveled from my core down my arms and out of my mark. Red and gold light filled the small garden, evolving the shine enveloping my body into a small sun. The pain in my shoulder evaporated, and afterwards I didn't feel anything except the light. I was always meant to be a being made of pure lightning, and I was tired, so tired of being told to suppress who I was.

"Jennifer! Don't!" His voice rang clear as he held a hand up over his eyes to block out my light. *I can hear again.* The light in his eyes was easier to see now, an unnatural vibrant green he kept hidden away, the gift he didn't want people to see. Everything was more obvious now. I saw and understood everything. He stepped back, away from me, but I was struck by the unexpected thought that he *should* fear me.

Everything should fear me.

My shoes lifted off the ground. I floated over the wall and landed on the soft earth of a garden in front of a small greenhouse. Marcus called my name, but it didn't matter. The Banshee had both Ashley and my sister. Whatever he had to say was irrelevant now.

There's nothing to fear anymore.

I reached for the doorknob and it melted into

putty between my fingers. The greenhouse door buckled from the heat and burst inward, scattering glass across the classroom. The little fragments spun in mid-air, frozen in their explosion. I floated by empty desks and plant supplies, barely aware of my surroundings as I traveled through the science room and out into the hall. My shoes trailed on the floor down the long corridor. They knocked against the stairs as I went up. The Banshee's light gave off a faint blue beacon in the dark, a lighthouse signaling the exact location where she hid—back where this all started, back where my journey in Savannah began.

Caution tape crisscrossed the doorway to Castlebury's room. Plastic sheets hung over the holes in the walls, and they waved in a non-existent wind. Dirty water puddled across the linoleum and fell upwards, ascending in little droplets to merge with dark stains freckling the ceiling. My golden light illuminated the world of gray, casting a glow like the morning sun. I reached for the caution tape. It withered away in the palm of my hand, exposing the broken door frame and the decimated classroom beyond. I brushed aside the plastic curtain, melting it away as I entered the room.

Like frozen dolls, students lay propped up against the back cabinets of broken beakers in a pretty little row. Webs of ice covered their bodies and sealed their cold eyelids shut. Becky lay with her head back at a weird angle, snowy icicles frosting her limp fingers. Her dead body leaned against Ashley's shoulder, but the cold hadn't settled over her limbs yet. Her chest rose and fell as if in sleep. *She's alive.*

I wasn't going to have one more person die because of me.

But where is my sister?

A figure hovered over the wet linoleum. He was short and mousy, and his glasses hung askew off the tip of his nose. The room was filled with shrapnel pieces of the rest of his body, blown apart from the center that held his ribcage and head. Part of an arm floated near his torso. One of his legs spun slowly around the orbit of his remains. It was as if a picture were captured of him in mid-explosion, a moment in time that would stand still forever.

Brent?

Behind the remains, someone cradled his head. Her bare feet dangled as her cotton dress billowed around her. *The Banshee.* She emitted a soft purple and blue color that reminded me of bioluminescent algae. An oval shape hung behind them in the middle of the air. A world of light and color—the land of the living—shined through the tear.

My breath caught in my throat as the power inside me wavered. *I made that tear. I created it when I gave the Wraith a body—when I killed Brent. The Banshee.* She escaped through the opening, drawn by the birth of the Wraith. Guilt tore at my power, sucking it dry like a desert laps up the rain.

My fault. My fault. MY FAULT.

My chin quivered as my power wavered like a defective light bulb.

No.

I couldn't dim.

I was going to save my sister and rip this Banshee apart!

She reached a pale hand for one of the frozen students sitting on the floor, a girl with familiar blonde hair that tumbled out of her messy bun. Caution tape wrapped around her hoodie with a protection sign on the front, tying her to the stool legs. Her freckled face hung limp to one side.

"Jacks?" My sister's head lolled as her eyes opened and searched the room for me.

"Release my sister." My voice boomed unnaturally, as though a goddess had issued a command from the heavens. Electric currents of red and gold fireworks crackled along the pattern of my gold mark as my hair rippled around my face.

The Banshee turned around, her throat opened, and a scream erupted from her neck to topple me. I waved my arm, brushing aside her scream. Her attack hit me with all the force of a wave crashing against a rocky shore, only I was the rock and the blast did nothing.

"Let her go," I said. My voice rumbled like

distant thunder.

She leapt at me, her fingernails out like claws.

"Enough," I said, and sent a golden punch of firelight whistling into her temple. Her transparent body skidded back across the water.

The Banshee staggered into an upturned desk, clutching the broken bits of her face which had started to solidify in her hands. She shrieked as her skin began the painful transformation into solid matter, into a living being.

"Jennifer!" Marcus said. He stood in the doorway, his salt knife out in front of him like a small sword. His shoulders slumped when he saw the Banshee. "What have you done?"

The Banshee grabbed my sister by the hair and dragged her out into the hall. Liz's cries of pain sent a guttural roar sweeping through my body. The desks flung off the floor, careening in every direction, clearing a path for me to follow.

"Never hurt someone I love ever again." I seized the ghost by her stupid neck.

She released my sister and pawed at her throat as the flesh stitched itself back together. The flesh formed a larynx and muscles and chin bones as my power flooded into her, giving the ghost a body. I squeezed her new neck hard as she struggled to breathe, and I caught myself savoring her anguish.

Good.

Any ghost who hurts the ones I love deserves all the pain my power can give.

Something collided with my gut so hard the wind knocked out of me. As I exhaled, I released the Banshee. It took a moment for my mind to catch up with what had happened to my body. Marcus leaned over me, his shoulder against mine, and all the air had gone out of me. He *punched* me. He had straight-up punched me in the stomach to get me to stop.

Gold light sparked around my body as I wheeled to hit him back, but he pulled my wrist and made me stagger forward. I fell into a table and tripped onto my knees.

The Banshee moaned with sorrow as she fled inside the classroom. She was changing rapidly from the neck down, her flesh spreading out from her collarbone to her ribcage. Marcus threw me his dirtiest look yet and used his salt knife to rip the caution tape off Liz.

"Come with me," he said, offering his hand. "We need to move quickly before the transformation finishes."

She took his hand. "Who the hell are you?"

"I need you to banish," he said as Marcus dragged Liz to the floating pieces of Brent.

The Banshee cradled his face lovingly in one hand and reached for my sister with the other. I used the table to prop myself back up. *Why did she want Liz so badly?* This was the first entity that hadn't gone after me, hadn't wanted another chance at living, but I was not the Sparrow it wanted. Liz had expelled the Poltergeist from me, but I still knew nothing about what she was *really* capable of.

"She wants to cross over," Marcus said to Liz. "Use your gift and release them."

The classroom glitched. The gray world pixelated, as if we stood inside a malfunctioning computer. Marcus gasped as the oval leading back to the land of the living fizzed and shrank a little. Something was wrong, and there was that humming sound again, like a million bees swarming in their hive.

"The Other," Marcus said, yelling to be heard over the buzzing. "It's collapsing. The Banshee made this with her pain and now that's disappearing, the tear is closing."

"No, please," the Banshee said with her new mouth. "My boy...my precious boy."

My boy? The Banshee. Brent.

The Banshee is Brent's *mother*?

Skin formed around her ribcage and grew down to her stomach and legs. A few seconds more and she would be alive. The tear leading to the land of the living collapsed in half.

"Please," the Banshee—Brent's mother— pleaded with Liz. "I can live again, but my son cannot. We just want to cross over. We just want to rest together...forever. Help us, Sparrow. Help us rest."

My sister looked over at me, her blue eyes electric with silver fire. Her power rippled with heat. *Is this what it's like to be near my power?*

I thought as Liz closed her eyes and reached for the Banshee. The room percussed with a clap of air and I fell upwards. Her light tore through the Other like a dying star, flooding the world with Liz's terrifying blaze. My stomach flipped up into my throat like the first drop on a roller coaster as I floated and came crashing back down. There was a popping sound and the floor came up fast, only I didn't hit the ground. I floated down slowly, as a leaf drifts to the forest floor. My shoes landed in a puddle, making a small ripple where I settled.

What just happened?

I turned around. We were back in the land of the living, and the classroom lay broken in full color. Liz stood a few feet away. She stared at the place where the hole used to be in the Other, but there was nothing there now. Her fists were still smoking.

I reached for her. "Hey. You okay?"

She turned around eyes dazed. "What... happened?"

"I don't know," I said. "You used your power."

"I know." Liz shook her head. "There was this pull, this voice inside of me. She told me to help her and her son cross over."

"The Banshee is obviously gone," Marcus snapped from behind me. He shook water off his jacket. "Don't you know what your sister can do?"

Liz and I exchanged confused glances.

"Why am I not surprised?" He huffed.

"*Banishment.* She can force any supernatural entity out of places they shouldn't be. Once banished, they are doomed to remain in the Other forever."

That's how she got rid of the Poltergeist.

He kicked an upturned desk with his boot. "God, I can't believe I didn't see the Banshee was Brent's mom. I thought it was just a ghost who escaped, but *no.* She was taking everyone close to Jennifer or had been close to her in order to find the Sparrow of Banishment. That's why she brought them here, where her son died. It all makes perfect sense, but I was so distracted by the destruction of two bumbling Sparrows, I didn't see it."

"Hey—" I started to say but he wheeled around and put a finger in my face.

"Don't start," he said. "This is because of you. When you ripped the Wraith out of him, she became a Banshee. She wanted to release her son from the pain *you* caused!"

I stepped back, unsure how to even respond. "But I didn't mean—"

"No," he said. "No, you don't get to defend yourself. I felt bad that your Dad abandoned you, left you here without explanation. *I did.* I even saved you when I shouldn't have, but she was right. Sparrows are always *reckless.* When your friends and family were taken, you acted without thinking. You turned the Banshee human without stopping to figure out why she was here in the first place."

"Hey," Liz said, stepping between us. "Back off! You don't get to talk to my sister that way. This isn't her fault and you know it."

"Jennifer?" Ashley's eyes fluttered awake as she lifted her head from her dead friend's shoulder. She smiled when she saw me, but that smile quickly disappeared. "Becky?" She grabbed her shoulders. Ashley's voice broke as she shook her hard and nothing happened.

Becky's head lolled to one side.

She was dead, and no amount of pleading or begging from Ashley was going to change that.

My power. I could bring ghosts back. Maybe I could bring people back too. I could finally do something good for a change. I reached for her cold hand and Marcus grabbed me by the wrist.

"Don't," Marcus spat in my face. "She's dead. It's too late. Once they've moved on, that's it. They're gone. No Sparrow could ever bring back someone who has died and crossed over. There's nothing you can do to make this right."

Ashley turned to me, and her features twisted with confusion and disbelief. "You did this? You're the reason the ghosts are here?

I backed away. "I...I didn't mean to."

My breath hitched as Marcus stepped between us. "She is why the Banshee was here, why the Wraith came, why Brent died, why almost everyone in our class was killed. She's the Sparrow of Summoning, a demon who wakes up other demons. All she does is leave a wake of destruction and pain wherever she goes."

"You killed my best friend?" Ashley bit her lip as she turned away from me, unable to look at me anymore. "Why did you come here?"

Only moments ago, she had kissed me, and now she looked like it was the worst decision she'd ever made in her entire life. I hadn't realized how much I had wanted her, how much from the moment I met her that I needed Ashley. Now, she was lost, and I would never feel the touch of her lips on mine again. What I had been given wasn't a gift at all. It was a curse.

I turned and ran. *Dad's journal.* The duffle bag lay by the entrance to the classroom. I didn't question how it got over there. I turned and grabbed it and tore out of the broken classroom, but I couldn't bring myself to see if Liz followed.

She told me more about her powers last night. Emily is the Sparrow of Summoning. She has the ability to give supernatural entities a body, but she says that if a demon possesses someone, and Emily touches him...she wouldn't elaborate, but I got the gist. Every time she does it, a gold mark appears on her arms. She calls it Equivalent Exchange. She's pulled over a little more into the Other every time. It's up to her chest now. We have to get rid of the mark before it consumes her, but she has no idea how.

There is something else. Part of her ability is controlled by will. If she wants, she can use her energy to attack ghosts and demons, even make them explode, but the effect is temporary. She won't elaborate on what will happen when both Sparrow powers are combined. It hurts too much to talk about her sister.

She wants to try to find the source of the curse to learn how to make the gold mark on her arms disappear. We heard there is a prophecy, and it's somewhere in New Orleans where her family—the Beaulieus—are from.

Here's hoping the city gives us some answers.

   Jacob
   April 30, 1991

15

Partings

Liz found me sitting on a bench under a street lamp in Johnson Square, my knees tucked under my chin as I held my duffle bag tightly in both hands. She walked over to my bench and sat down beside me, not saying a word. For a while we sat there watching water spill over in the fountain in the center of the square. Fireflies winked in and out of the bushes beneath the giant oaks. The moon hung in the sky, almost full. She said nothing until an ambulance and police cars arrived in front of Northwinds, and then nodded at me like we should probably make ourselves scarce. I followed Liz away from Johnson Square down Bull Street.

"We're only a block or so away from Marshall

House," Liz said. "No one knows we're here, which should give us time if the cops go looking for us. That is, if Ashley and Marcus tell them the truth, which I doubt."

We passed through a shadow created by the awning of a jewelry store and turned left at East Broughton Street. When Johnson Square was completely out of sight, I burst into fresh tears.

"It's *my* fault. It's all my fault." I dropped to my knees, not caring that I kneeled in the middle of the sidewalk blocking everyone.

Liz didn't hesitate. She caught me on the way down. As she held me in her arms and let me cry as long as I wanted. I let myself feel everything I had been holding back the last few days—Dad's disappearance, Brent's death, Marcus's angry words, Becky's death, and Ashley's hurt face. That last image hurt most of all. A person or two passed by us, but she shooed them away. When I'd finally finished hyperventilating, Liz took my face in both hands.

"Don't you listen to him," she said. "I don't care what your power is or what has happened or even how many people have died. None of this was your fault. You don't have to internalize the garbage someone else throws out. I don't care what he says. We helped release that boy from the torture. We sent the Banshee and her son to a better place."

"You did that," I sniffed. "You, not me. I'm the reason Brent was all exploded like that. That was Brent, the boy I ripped the Wraith out of. I'm the one with the garbage power. I don't know what Dad was thinking. He said if I wanted to, I could use my power for good, but that was a lie just like everything else he's ever said. They were just empty words to make me feel better about having the worst power in all of existence."

She grabbed me by the chin and forced me to look at her. "You do not have a garbage power. And you can help people. I read Dad's journal. What if a ghost had been murdered? Wrongly killed? You could give them a second chance. You could bring them back. That is not a bad power, it's just being used in the wrong ways for the wrong reasons. And I could end up banishing someone innocent that didn't deserve it. You see? Power isn't about good or bad—it's how you use it."

She handed me a tissue from her pocket, and I used it to wipe my runny nose. I thought over everything she had said. As much as I hated to admit it, she was right. Still, it didn't make me feel any better about the people I did kill nor erase from my mind the way Marcus and Ashley had looked at me.

"Listen," Liz said. "Let's go back to the hotel, get a good night's sleep, and attack this problem in the morning. I will set up some wards and we will be safe, I swear. Tomorrow, we look for Dad."

"Blackwell Antiques." I blurted it out without thinking. "I never found out where it is."

She blinked at me. "Did you not find out at

the library?"

"I couldn't log into the internet," I explained. "Can you Google it with your phone? I'm sure that's where they're keeping Dad. That guy who made you banish the Banshee. That's Marcus, and right before the ghost attacked, he admitted he's Arturo's grandson."

"What?" Liz shouted and a woman in a pink shirt paused to stare at her.

"Keep your voice down," I hissed.

"That would explain why we haven't heard from him," Liz whispered. "We could try and break in, solve both problems in one go: find the necklace, find Dad, find Miriam. So, three things." Liz searched on her phone for Blackwell Antiques.

"You're right," she said, shutting her phone. "It's over on River Street. Not that far. I don't think we should go tonight. That was enough for one day."

"Yeah," she said solemnly. "I'm pretty beat, myself. By the way, where is my bag?"

I shook my head. "I couldn't find it when the Banshee took you." I unzipped my duffle bag and pulled out her bat. "But I did grab this."

She took it from me and kissed my cheek. "That was exactly what I needed. Thank you. I left it back in the classroom, I guess. Everything happened so quickly. I heard the screams and came running and then...well, no use reliving the rest."

"Can we go?" I said. "I'm tired."

"Me too," she said. "I'm not looking forward

to going back to that hotel with those ghosts running all over the place, but as long as we have wards set up, we should be fine. Let's go. Rest will do us both some good."

I nodded, not wanting to say anything else right then. As I followed Liz down the street back inside the entrance of the Marshall House, I couldn't stop torturing myself with images of Ashley's face. She hated me now. *Really* hated me. I'd killed her best friend, and no matter what Liz said to comfort me, Marcus was right. There was no way I could take that back.

CAT SCULLY

We found the prophecy.

It's more horrible than we expected.

Emily hasn't spoken since we left New Orleans. We need to find a place to hide out, some place Emily can try to learn to control her powers in peace. My family has an old farmland no one uses. We're heading there now.

Jacob
May 5, 1991

16

The Drawing

WE RETURNED TO THE hotel lobby and made it through without any word from Gary. He could see we had been through hell and we were in no mood to talk about it, but I made sure to return the little wave he gave us anyway. We headed up the elevator and down the hall back to our room, but I kept checking over my shoulder for the Confederate soldier or the little girl ghosts. There was nothing. The wards on our jacket and pullover were working. When we got inside, as I watched Liz put up drawings of wards around the room, little by little, my body relaxed.

I spent way too much time in the shower thinking about Marcus, how much I hated him, how much I just wanted him to burn. His grandmother Miriam had probably taken Dad and trapped him in Blackwell Antiques, and Marcus probably knew this whole time. I don't know why I ever trusted him, why I thought it would ever be an innovative idea to be so close to him in the library. Never again.

I threw on my pajamas and climbed into bed, not caring that my hair was still wet. Liz was already out cold, not even having bothered with the shower. She was the last thing I saw before I closed my eyes. We slept for an unknowable amount of time. If I dreamt of anything, I don't remember it. Sleeping was a series of terrible dreams, melting into bathroom breaks, then back into sleep again. I didn't wake until a knock came at the door.

Liz flicked on the light. "I'm coming," she called.

I blinked awake and tried to ignore that my head felt about the size of a dirigible balloon.

She opened it enough to see out, leaving the latch still hitched. "What is it?"

"Housekeeping," a female voice said.

"Oh, sure." Liz scratched her shorts until her wedgie finally came loose. "Could you give us an hour?"

"Absolutely," she said and left.

Liz shut the door and shuffled back to bed, flopping face-down on the pillows. She let out a groan that sounded more like air being let out of a tire than any sound actual humans make.

"What time is it?" I said, rolling over. My shirt

had stuck to my back with sweat. I had to peel it off to convince my clothes to let me go.

She lifted her head and snatched her phone from the charger on the hardwood desk next to her bed. "7:30. We better get dressed."

I stretched until my spine popped and curled back into my stomach.

"Do you want to take the first shower?" she offered.

I crawled my way out of the sheets. "No, it's fine. You go first."

She pulled her hair out of a bun and sniffed the end of it. "I smell horrible. I'll probably have to take two showers."

I grinned. "With the firecracker that combed my hair, I probably need three."

"After that, breakfast." She laughed as she stumbled over to the bathroom. "We're going to need a big one if we're infiltrating the antique store. I won't leave until I annihilate the biggest stack of pancakes you've ever seen."

Liz shut the door gently behind her. When the water turned on, I climbed out of bed and opened the curtains to let in some light. I had spent a lot of time in the dark the past few days. It was nice to let in some morning sunlight. I watched the traffic on the street below. Savannah was awake and already moving. For such a small town, it seemed to never sleep. The joggers and baby walkers and business people with their lattes were already out in full force along the sidewalks. I leaned out the window and found the enormous SCAD sign was just down the road. We weren't that far from Jen Library. I hadn't realized in all the chaos.

Dad's journal. I should probably read the rest of it before we leave.

I retrieved the journal from my duffle bag and ran my hands across the soft leather. Over the past few days, the size of it seemed to grow in my mind, until it weighed as much as a dictionary or one of those coffee table art books. Now, sitting on a bed that wasn't mine, the journal was much smaller than I remembered.

I brought the book to my nose. The tea-stained pages smelled like him, like Earl Grey tea and whiskey from the decanter he kept in his office. My heart ached for him, and I hated myself for feeling longing for a person that I loved who had screwed me over so royally. I flipped through his hand-scribbled notes, drawings, charts, symbols... everything. Page after page classified each entity by type, difficulty, warnings, and weakness along with an illustrated picture. I read the entry that listed the definition of a ghost versus a demon again. I flipped through the Banshee, Wraith, Phantom, and Poltergeist. I read the Ghoul, the Howler, the Plague, the Eyes, and the vague writing about the Beast. I stopped on the drawing of Miriam and Arturo. I hadn't gotten that deep into the book yet, hadn't read how Mom and Dad's story ended because I still felt terrible that the water in the classroom had damaged it. Arturo looked a bit like Doctor Strange with thick, black eyebrows and a goatee. Miriam had sharp cheek bones and a long braid of hair that hung over one shoulder. Both of them were extraordinarily good looking, like they could have been cover models on a goth magazine. They were not what I had pictured at all.

Something small fell out of the book and fluttered to the ground like a moth's wing. It was yellowed parchment paper, worn along the edges, and folded over multiple times. I picked it up by its corner and unfolded the drawing with care. It was a picture of a graveyard, sketched by hand in pen so hastily the lines had smudged. Mom was clearly distressed when she drew this. This image had the same style as her Wraith and Poltergeist drawings, but the lines were more erratic and spread out all over the place. Dark bodies spiraled out of an ironwork gate. Wisps of ghosts with hollow pits for eyes rose out of open tombs. Skeletal hands parted the earth and clawed at the sky, desperate to break the surface. Two girls stood at the center of the graveyard, their dark hair lifting all around them. Their pale arms embraced the stars as they opened a giant, black gate. At the bottom, written in sweeping black pen were the words:

Do Not Open the Gate.

The water turned off inside the shower.

"You know," Liz said, loud enough so I could

hear her from inside the bathroom. "I think this could be it. Today could be the day we save Dad, find the necklace, and maybe even get our normal lives back."

A few moments later, the bathroom door swung open and revealed Liz fully dressed. Her usual messy bun was piled high and tight on her head. She was in her favorite shirt, a black crop top with bold, white letters that read: "Fight!" Her waist-high jeans met just where the shirt ended.

I closed the journal but kept the paper in my hands. "Do you remember Dad's library?"

"You mean the one in the basement?" she said.

"The room he always kept locked, the one he never let us in."

She stuck a toothbrush in her mouth. "Of course, I do. He spent hours in there. I tried to kick the door down more than once."

"Do you remember the day you unlocked the door?" I said.

She paused, eyes racing back and forth as they did every time she shuffled through memories. "Yes. I found the key to his office in his sock drawer. I went down to the basement and he caught me. You had made me take you along."

The memory knocked the wind out of my chest. I shivered and rubbed my hands against my arms to stop the goosebumps. I saw the mark and stopped. It had grown from using my power on the Banshee and I hadn't noticed. Now it had spread to meet in the middle of my chest, forming finger-like patterns over my ribcage. I shook to make the fear go away, but it didn't work.

"Don't worry," she said and sat on the bed next to me. "We'll figure out how to get rid of that mark. I'm sure there will be something in Blackwell Antiques with the answer. Or we'll find Dad and he'll tell us. Why were you asking me about that day in the basement?"

I sighed, not wanting to remember, but I had to. It was important. "Do you remember what we found?" I said.

"A book," she said. "I remember the cover. It was old, wrapped in fabric the way all old books are. I hate thinking about it. There were pictures of orange eyes in dark windows, women floating down a staircase, outlines of men in white wigs and buckled shoes against headstones. Gives me shivers."

I nodded. "All this time, I thought he was collecting research for his job, but he wasn't. He was researching legends about the Sparrow. He and Mom were looking for a prophecy and he found one." I handed her the drawing.

She ran her fingers over the ink of the ghosts, the headstones, the two girls standing beside a black gate. "What is this?"

"Mom drew it," I said. "Remember how they had said they traveled to New Orleans because they were researching the origin of the Sparrow powers and how to stop them? They found a prophecy but said something about it being worse than they had imagined. I think this is it. I mean, what else could it be?"

She leaned closer. "Whoever drew this prophecy, I don't know what it's implying, other than a Sparrow should not open this gate, but there is something about it that bothers me more. I know where this is. The obelisk, the angels, the tombs—It's Bonaventure."

"What is Bonaventure?" I said.

"The largest graveyard in Savannah," Liz said. "It's outside of town and spread out over 160 acres. There are hundreds of people buried there. If one or both of us were able to open the Black Gate there, it would rip a hole so big, the dead would flood the living. It's large enough that some folks call Bonaventure a 'town of the dead.'"

I traced my finger over the necklace, unable to stop the obvious question from skipping over and over my thoughts like stones tossed across a pond. "What does the gate do?"

"Wish I knew. Maybe it's whatever Arturo was trying to accomplish by combining the Sparrow powers." She tapped at the girls' necks. "They're both wearing a necklace."

I frowned. "Do you think they're Obsidian necklaces? Dad only ever talked about one."

"Well," Liz said, "maybe there is more than one."

She remembered the toothbrush in her mouth and brushed furiously as she headed back to the bathroom. When she came back out again, she shook her head. "I'm sorry for what I said. I didn't mean to make you feel like you couldn't stay with me."

I twirled a strand of hair between my fingers. "I miss him, and I hate him. I just want to see Dad again. I just want to know he's okay."

She rubbed my shoulder. "Don't worry. We'll go downstairs, have some breakfast. We'll go to Blackwell Antiques and we will find him. You know how I know?"

"How?" I said.

"Because we're together on this." She smiled. "Whatever happens, I promise I'm going to be there for you from now on. We've had a scary couple of days. I don't know anything about my powers, and you don't know anything about yours, but I'm happy you and I are talking again. If we're together, what can go wrong?"

We've had peace for a little while now.

Emily suggested we get married. I agreed, but then she said we should share my journal with any children we might have. I can't live without her, but I can't picture wanting children to enter into a life as hard as ours has been. Passing down the mysteries of her curse is not an exact science, but it seems inevitable.

Maybe it's because I've been studying for exams. College is harder than I thought, but I like it. I think I have a knack for historical journalism. Learning about the past might help us figure out the future. The more I learn, the more I can help her. Maybe when I get my P.H.D. Maybe then I'll be prepared enough to even consider having children.

She keeps studying that prophecy day and night. With all of her drawings, maybe she should go after a career in art. Anything would be better than studying that drawing all day.

Jacob
April 12, 1995

17

Antiques

My breath wheezed in and out as I raced to catch up with Liz. She was already halfway down the sidewalk and the breakfast I had scarfed down sloshed around in my stomach. My gut churned somewhere between nervous butterflies and full-on panic attack. I tried to stifle the smile on my face. Today could be the day. We could get rid of my mark, get Dad back, find out how to stop the prophecy of the Black Gate—everything.

The sun was out, bright in a cloudless sky, as if yesterday's rain had never happened. The heat had already evaporated most of the water off the sidewalks and taken away most of the puddles in the roads between our hotel and River Street. I enjoyed every bit of it because this beautiful day was fleeting. We would be flooded again by afternoon, give or take.

"Hurry," Liz called over her shoulder. "It's already 9:02."

"I'm trying!" I yelled back. "I'm still sore from yesterday! Are we going to rest ever?"

"Not until we're dead," Liz replied.

We wound our way down the hill towards Blackwell Antiques over on River Street. The crowds of pedestrians walking dogs or small children multiplied as we got closer. We reached the familiar dome of City Hall; whose shining gold paint was particularly bright today. River Street lay just beyond, according to Google Maps, but I didn't understand how it could be one story down from the main street level.

The famous red lion and Cotton Exchange building lay ahead. Liz told me small flights of stone staircases to River Street lay just beneath every twenty feet or so. She said Savannah hid its illusions well, including the fact the entire portion of the city along the river was built on stilts. I couldn't picture what she was describing at all, but I gave her the thumbs up so she would stop talking about it and we could just get going.

"There it is," Liz said, pointing to a cluster of shops on the other side of the road. "River Street."

We approached a hanging bridge and metal walkways from East Bay Street that connected to the strips of brick-and-mortar shops. They made the buildings look like they were only two stories high when, in actuality, they were about four. The bridges allowed the third floor to function as a series of shops facing East Bay, and the first floor facing the river to be a completely separate set of shops.

"Quirky and unique with a big old dash of southern charm," I said. "That's Savannah for you."

Liz raised her eyebrow. "You sure are taking a liking to it here."

I shrugged. "After a week of being chased by horrible monsters, I'm learning to appreciate the little things."

As we reached one of the narrow bridges, I shivered. Goosebumps ran up the backs of my arms. "Hey, Liz? There's something beneath our feet, and it certainly isn't alive. I can feel the dead pulling me."

"I feel it too," Liz said, as if reading my thoughts. "Let's keep moving."

I held tight onto the handrail as we crossed the metal bridge, reminded of how much I hated heights. The further we traveled across the bridge, the more the feeling that the dead watched us dissipated. A "Blackwell Antiques" sign swung in the sunlight. Beneath it was another shop, a hand with an eye in its center painted on the blacked-out glass window sat with the words, "Divinations and Spirit Consultations." Blackwell Antiques seemed to be the one exception to the series of shops—one owner managed all the floors.

A "Closed for Renovations" sign hung on the door and all the lights were off.

"Are you sure you want to do this?" I asked Liz as we approached the front door. "This place makes me feel weird, and not in the 'I just walked over a bunch of dead people' way."

"Not really," she said. "But what other choice do we have? Let's go inside, see what Marcus and Miriam keep in her basement on the Sparrows—including Dad—and then get the heck out of here." Liz peered in the tinted windows. "I don't see anyone. They're probably out looking for us."

"Should we try the door?" I said.

She turned the handle. "It's open. So much for home security."

A little bell chimed as she pushed the door in. Fresh wood lacquer fumes and paint primer smacked me square in the nose. I fanned the smell away, but it was strong. The gesture did nothing but spread it around more. "God, it reeks," I said. "Guess that sign wasn't just for show. They really are doing renovations. You'd think they'd air out the place."

"Whoa," Liz said, "this place is incredible."

We stood in the entrance to a gigantic open room that felt more like a warehouse than a quaint little shop. The furniture stacked wall-to-wall, so tightly we couldn't walk. The high cabinets were crafted out of rosy-brown wood. Glass displays held rows of turquoise stones and abandoned diamond rings. Racks of antique dresses filled every last inch of space. In the center of the maze sat a trio of dancing fountain girls. The surrounding tile floor was the only area in the entire place where there was open room to walk. The girls' serene stone faces gazed over baskets draped on their arms; water cascaded into the circular basin at their sandaled feet.

"I think the front counter is over here," Liz said.

She squeezed through cabinets of jewelry, and I went in after her. Behind the glass, large rings with ornate jewels, small diamonds in forgotten wedding rings, and resplendent necklaces on the necks of porcelain busts dazzled me.

"Where do you think she got all of this stuff?" I said. "It's gorgeous."

"I wouldn't get too close," Liz said. "They're probably haunted as hell. The jewels have the same sort of sick feeling as the Banshee and Poltergeist coming off them."

"Really?" I said. "I don't feel anything. Looks like you have another power I don't, like how you heard those ghost girls at Marshall House, but I didn't. You seem to be more sensitive."

She shrugged. "Guess so."

"Do any of these look like the Obsidian necklace?" I asked.

She surveyed the glass and dazzling jewels inside. "No. None of these look remotely like what we'd be looking for. Obsidian is black and smooth and reflects almost no light when it's cut."

"I'm sweating in this." I unzipped my hoodie.

The gold on my neck glittered off the jewelry pieces. "I can't deal with hiding it anymore."

"Why were you hiding it in the first place?" Liz said. "No one can see it but us."

I rolled my eyes. "I don't know. It made me feel better. How do we get downstairs, anyway?"

"Through there, I guess?" Liz gestured to a narrow passage between a china cabinet and bookshelf.

I followed her down the aisle, keeping my elbows in. The fumes made my head swim and I wobbled, knocking into one of the wardrobes covered in chalky blue paint. If I could make it one day without one billion injuries, I might just make it out of this entire ordeal alive.

We reached the end of the maze and stopped at a small clearing in front of a red door as cracked and old as the brick walls. I checked my pants and arms, elbows, and hair—no paint. Liz had some just above her left elbow though, white and smeared up her arm. When I pointed it out, she let out a groan.

"Did they have to stick freshly painted pieces in that maze?" she said.

I shrugged.

I tried the door handle and found it unlocked, so I pushed it open. The flight of stairs leading down were lit by gas lamps. A distant light glowed at the bottom of the steps.

"Wow," I said. "It's so dingy down there."

Liz touched my arm. "Do you think it's safe?

Maybe we should wait..."

"Why?" I said. "They're not here and we're probably not going to get a better chance than this one."

She sighed. "You're right. At least let me go first."

I kept close to her, one or two steps behind. In such an old house, I expected each step to creak with our descent, but they didn't. The carpet muffled any noise our shoes might make. Flaking wallpaper curled where wood met brick. Just like Northwinds, the stairwell smelled like cedar and smoky red brick dust. Spray painted over the exposed brick areas were symbols, lines with runes and evil eyes, cursive words written in a language I couldn't read or even attempt to understand. It was hard to focus on walking with so many symbols weaving and overlapping each other, every one of them so beautiful.

We reached the bottom and entered a long hallway with four closed white doors set in paisley brown wallpaper that shimmered in the lamp light. The door at the end of the hall was open. Liz flicked on the hall light.

"Whoa," she said. "This is nuts. Look at all of these."

No. It wasn't the wallpaper that was shimmering. A thousand small picture frames covered every inch of free space, all varying in size from a square Polaroid to a standard photo print to larger portraits.

"What are all of these?" I said.

"Former clients," Liz said, pointing to an inscription beneath a photo. "Seems Miriam likes to keep a memento of each house their family has cleaned."

I drew closer to a picture of two Goth teens, a guy with straight hair and a girl with heavy eyeliner and black lipstick, hands deep in their pockets as they stood in front of a house. The bottom of the frame read Salem, Mass. "I can see that."

"We need to keep moving," she said.

There were so many pictures it was hard to focus on just one as we passed them all. There were families with girls in bell bottom jeans, surly teens in distressed leather, stern mothers with crosses round their necks. Their fingers pressed hard into their children's shoulders as they posed. There were people of every age, every era. There were even women in Victorian lace and corsets, women in colonial dresses of simple linen, men with muskets, and children in white wigs.

"Just how long has their family been doing this?" I said.

"I'm not sure." Liz glanced at a photo and froze. She grabbed my hand and pointed at the Polaroid. There, among the many frames, two girls stood with their arms entwined in muted color. The tallest girl was fair, hair almost white against the backdrop of trees and rose bushes. The shorter was freckled, and even with the grain, her hair was a fire the camera lens could not dampen. I'd seen her gray eyes all my life. My hand covered my mouth as I gasped.

Liz pointed at the photo. "Mom, and Amelia. Wow. We look just like them."

"So, Dad wasn't lying," I said. "They really did live with Arturo before."

We continued down the hall, both of us shaken. It was one thing to read all of this in Dad's journal, another to see the truth for ourselves. Liz opened the next door at the end of the hall, only this one was painted a particular shade called "Haint blue" that was believed to keep the spirits out. We entered a room not much bigger than Dad's study. Bookshelves lined the walls, and where there wasn't a bookshelf, the walls were filled with paintings of angels fighting demons. Clusters of drying herbs hung from the ceiling. Jars of pickled eyeballs floated in yellow juice. Skulls of wolves and bats, cats and snakes lined the tops of the bookshelves. Crystals varying in size from my fist to my head functioned as bookends.

"This must be the conjuring parlor Dad mentioned," Liz said.

"Sure, looks like it," I said.

On the opposite side of the room sat a floor-length mirror, but the fabric draped over it had fallen to one side. Instead of a blank glass that reflected the room, its glossy surface was completely black.

"What is that?" Liz said.

"Wait. I think it's the Mirror Door." I reached to touch it. "I think this is it."

My hand wiped away the silk fabric. It glided to the floor with the slow grace of a butterfly's wing. The onyx surface did not reflect even the smallest light. It was like gazing into a tar pit, devoid of all light and color, only to find yourself looking back. There was something in that mirror. The closer I got, the more the mark on my body glowed. The flames bounced off every shiny surface in the parlor—the jars, the pictures, the statues— everything but the mirror. The clean, smooth glass swallowed all light, an oval black hole.

I placed a hand on the cold surface. Everything around my hand rippled and pulsed. "It's a door to the Other. This is what Arturo made Mom and Aunt Amelia create."

The doorknob leading to the back room turned and my heart stopped. A woman stood in the doorway, dressed all in black from her boots to the lace wrapped around her neck. Layers upon layers of fine fabric fit against her body in exacting cuts of Victorian style. She played with a bead on her necklace at the end of a long gold chain, but it wasn't just a bead—it was a black crystal in the shape of a Scarab beetle with a skull for a face. A lone pearl dangled from its bottom legs. It could only be one thing—The Obsidian necklace.

"Hello, Sparrows. I'm Miriam Blackwood. Welcome to my home."

18

Miriam

"Hello, Miriam," I said.

Liz took my hand in hers as Miriam glided into the room. She was even lovelier than Dad's journal implied. Her graceful steps made the dress whisper around her ankles. There was no way in hell this woman was Marcus's grandmother. No wrinkles, smooth cheeks with a healthy pink glow, and perfect white teeth when she smiled. A pearl and emerald comb adorned her full, brunette hair which flowed in a loose braid over one shoulder. I didn't know a lot about how women aged or what they should or should not look like, and I didn't really care, but there was no universe where this woman was older than forty. As she took me in with a lifted chin, I observed that her eyes were far too old, too wise, to belong to a younger woman.

"Welcome." Her Southern accent was so much deeper than I anticipated, like she wanted to lull me right to sleep by just talking. "I'm glad we finally have a chance to speak with one another. Please. Have a seat."

She gestured to the chairs around the table in the center of the room. Liz and I exchanged looks, both of us unsure whether this woman was going to serve us tea and biscuits or make us eat someone's heart. When dealing with a woman who bore a striking resemblance to a viper in a Victorian dress, there was no middle option.

Liz and I took the plain wooden seats opposite the high-backed chair and waited for Miriam to join us, but she did not. Instead, she flipped the light switch, but no overhead light came on. Locks snapped over my wrists and wound around my ankles. I twisted my arm and kicked as hard as I could, but the chair only wobbled. *Damnit.*

The door opened again as Marcus emerged from the hallway wearing his jean jacket again and a t-shirt from the band Ghost, but his hair was full of mousse or something because it was the tidiest I'd ever seen it.

Miriam waved her hand. "You may lock the door."

Liz spat at him, "Stay away from us."

Marcus did as he was asked, and his eyes were cold as turned to address us. "Hello, Sparrows.

How good to see you again after you abandoned Ashley and left her to deal with the body of her dead friend, alone."

"I'm sorry," he said, tone flat. "But you two are a danger to everyone. We can't have you running free anymore."

I couldn't look at him.

"Marcus is right. This is the only way." Miriam turned her attention away from him back to Liz and me. "Tell me, Sparrow of Summoning, does it burn yet? I'm sure the pain has only gotten worse." Miriam's voice was soft and husky, like running your hand across silk sheets.

"No. I'm perfectly fine."

She smiled and smoothed the lines of her dress. Now that she sat closer, I could pick out the embroidery in the fabric, birds eating worms, snakes devouring birds. *Of course. Why did I expect anything else?*

"Your mother and her sister were students here once. My beloved Arturo trained them to control their impulses, use their gifts to rid people's homes of nasty spirits, banish demons from people's bodies—use their terrible powers for good. Then your father stole the Sparrows away." Her fist clenched for a moment, but she caught herself and turned her attention to untying a velvet bag in the center of the table instead.

"Whatever," Liz said. "Don't try and spin this into something it's not. You're not the hero here. You want to trap us just like you did with our mother."

"Is that what you believe?" Miriam shuffled her tarot cards in her long fingers. "I'm not evil, but you my dear are not exactly good. Can you honestly say your untrained gift has helped those around you? Or have your gifts caused only death and destruction wherever you go? An undisciplined Sparrow bleeds the line between the dead and the living into the living with reckless abandon, but with proper control, your power can be used for good."

That's exactly what Dad had said. I thought he meant we could help people, like how we helped the Banshee cross over. *What good was my power?* I could give ghosts a second chance at life, but from what I learned from Dad's journal most ghosts aren't like the Banshee. They don't want to be reunited with a loved one in the hereafter. They are trapped in the Other, doomed to repeat their own personal hells, and all they want is out.

Miriam spread the cards across the table in a great arc. "Sparrow of Summoning, Marcus tells me you resurrected not one, not two, but three spirits in a matter of days." She flipped over a card of a female knight holding an enormous sword while crimson fire engulfed her fists. The words "Knight of Swords" ran along the bottom. "There's fire, so much fire in your soul. You long to be the one saving everyone, but you're doomed to carry the same power as the flame—the light of destruction."

"I'm not destructive," I snapped at her. "And I'm not doomed. Your stupid cards don't mean anything."

"Sparrow of Banishment," she continued. "Your power is also taking its toll now, Elizabeth Strange." She flipped a second card from the arc. This time it was the "Knight of Cups" with a silver knight lifting up a golden chalice in her hands to the heavens. "Your silver mark will devour you. Out of the pair, you are the more emotional one. You feel so deeply the loss of your mother and so strongly the desire to protect your sister, but both are a fool's errand."

Liz blushed. "I didn't want Jennifer to know about my mark."

"It's okay, Liz. I knew." I turned to Miriam. "What are you getting at? Besides some boring card tricks?"

Miriam collected the cards back into the security of her hands. "Use your gift of Summoning to return Arturo to me, and I will rid you of your marks."

I raised an eyebrow. "How?"

"First, a favor." She flipped up a card. It was a painting of a brick tower and two girls crashing down to the ground as lightning struck. "I sent the spirits to find you. I needed you awake to resurrect Arturo and finish his magnificent work—*our* great work. The world is full of spirits and it needs a proper cleansing. With your help, living and training here, you will be able to use your powers for good. Elizabeth, you can banish ghosts that infest people's homes like flies and force them to cross the veil. Jennifer, you can burst the demons before they're able to possess children and give life back to those who truly deserve a second chance. Together, you demons *can* do good. That was Arturo's belief."

"But wait," Liz said. "All of the jewels upstairs were haunted. Are you selling haunted artifacts to people and then collecting on both the sale and the so-called cleansing?"

My eyes widened. The articles. The allegations. *So that's why people called the Blackwell family a bunch of criminals.*

"You're not helping people," I said. "You're infecting them and then coming to collect. Bet you couldn't sustain that business practice for long."

Her porcelain face cracked, putting a dent in her perfect makeup. She got up from her seat and slid across the darkened parlor like a ship parting the water. The mirror greeted her without reflection, a shiny and hollow door yawning out into the Other. She caressed the smooth glass with the back of her hand like she would tease a lover. "I see you found my Mirror Door. It's as beautiful as the day Emily and Amelia forged it with their powers. You two can do such wonderful things when you're together, but even such a wonderful treasure is only a half measure compared to what you two are truly capable of."

"Arturo. Come to me," she crooned out into the emptiness of the black pit. "Your birds are safe in their nest and would like you to come home."

Every picture frame shook on its nail. The incandescent lights went out. The gas lamps flickered, casting long shadows on Miriam's face, revealing every wrinkle she had somehow concealed. Something rose in the onyx mirror's darkness, a form growing. The surface pulsed as if a stone had been thrown into a pond as the entity inside took shape. A skull pressed its face out of the ink. Red eyes opened and drank in every detail of the room, finally resting on Liz and me. It grinned at us with a mouth full of black teeth.

"Sparrows." His voice echoed with the deepest, richest Savannah accent I'd ever heard. "I've so been looking forward to meeting the latest editions."

The skull pushed out of the ether followed by muscular shoulders, long arms, big hands—obviously, a ghost of someone who lived rather than a misshapen demon. His form was a lot like the Banshee in the way that his outline was delicate around the edges. When he moved, his footsteps would jerk in the wrong direction, but it was clearly the man from Mom's drawing.

Miriam led him to our table with a beckoning finger, placing a hand on my shoulder. "This is the one."

Arturo's ghost got down on one knee like he

was proposing. "Sparrow of Summoning, would you be so kind as to give me a body."

I glanced at Marcus. He leaned against the wall by the door, arms crossed, and he was trying for all the world not to watch what was taking place ten feet away. His eyes met mine. I bit my lip to keep from crying. Marcus could do something to help us, but instead he stood in the doorway doing nothing like the goddamn coward he was. I couldn't stand to look at him for one more second. I closed my eyes and waited for the inevitable.

"Don't worry." Arturo's whisper against my ear was so very cold. "It will all be over in a moment."

The fire started in my left arm. I kept my eyes shut, but I couldn't stop the volcanic heat from coursing down my arms and flooding into Arturo. It flowed as my head swam. I opened my eyes to find Marcus standing behind Miriam with one of her crystal balls held above his head. The orb hit her head with a gigantic crack and her body folded into a pile of fabric at my feet. He ignored me, searched her clothes as fast as he could. I gaped as he retrieved the salt knife, but it was too late. Arturo sighed into existence and let me go. Black filled the corners of my vision as my skin ran hot and cold.

Marcus leapt to his feet, knife ready in his hand, but his eyes were wide with defeat. "Father. Don't do this."

Father?

Arturo was even bigger alive than as a ghost,

but far more glamorous than in Mom's drawing. Like Miriam, his attire was straight out of the Victorian era. His black shirt was tucked into tailored gray slacks beneath a velvet waistcoat. The greatcoat he wore reached down to his knees and was made of similar material to Miriam's dress, with snakes coiling up the lapels to devour birds around his collar. His black hair and heavy eyebrows brought out the intensity of his blue eyes as he turned to his son.

"Don't you want to see your father return?" he said and back-handed Marcus across the room and over Miriam's high-backed chair.

My thoughts swam as I tried to process what Marcus was doing, why he was fighting this. He got back to his feet, took a swing at Arturo, and missed. His father punched his son in the throat and sent him down to the ground.

"I had high hopes for you, my boy," he said. "Hopefully when you wake, you'll come to your senses and we can put this whole nasty scuffle behind us in favor of greater pursuits." Arturo inspected the journal as he kneeled to pick up the salt knife where Marcus had dropped it.

He turned back to address me. "Thank you, darlin'. You've released me from my unfortunate prison. I can't thank you enough." He held a hand out to me and soon retracted it when he figured out, I was still bound to the chair. "I'm Belasco. Arturo Maxwell Belasco if you want the full credentials, and Art if you want to keep things informal. However, since we are new acquaintances and not old friends, forgive me if I prefer Arturo until we get to know each other better. And we *will* be getting to know each other better, won't we, Sparrows?" That last part he addressed to both of us with a big, performer grin.

Liz spit at him. "We're not going to help you."

Arturo laughed. "I like a Sparrow with a lot of fight in her. This one is full of spit and vinegar, a trait she no doubt inherited from her father." Arturo bowed deeply to her. "Sparrow of Banishment. Pleased as ever to meet you. Wouldn't want you to feel left out from our little party. Speaking of fathers, why don't we have a little family reunion? Must say our goodbyes before we send him to the great beyond."

"What do you mean?" Liz said.

Black snuck in and danced around the corners of my vision.

"Why, didn't Miriam tell you?" he said coolly. "Your father is here. We couldn't have him getting out and running away with our Sparrows again, could we? We kept him safe...for now. I mean to train you, Sparrows, but we can discuss the details of that later."

I blinked to try and stay awake but bringing Arturo back had drained too much out of me. My head sank to my chest.

"No, Jacks!" Liz cried. "Stay with me. Please. Don't pass out. Don't leave me!"

"Oh, quit your yapping," he said as he grabbed

my chair and dragged it towards the door on the far side of the room. "She's not crossing over, she's passing out. She needs to recharge for the big night, and you two can rest up fine in one of the cells. We usually keep them on reserve for the possessed in need of an exorcism."

I struggled to stay awake as he unlocked the door with a heavy key and pulled me into a back room that reeked of sawdust and salty fear. My vision faded as Arturo continued to pull me in small bursts past cells with iron bars and little ratty beds on weak bed frames. My eyes closed as he shut my cell door with a clank.

"Sweet dreams, Sparrow. I'll see you when you wake."

Liz screamed as he went back out into the parlor and it was the last sound I heard before everything drifted into black.

19

Onyx

A DROPLET OF WATER hit my face, waking me. I went to wipe it and couldn't lift my hand. My arms were bound to my sides. I must have passed out after they put me in the cell. *The chair. I'm still strapped to it, but I'm not wearing my hoodie.* It had been cut off and lay in pieces around the sawdust floor. I wasn't protected anymore.

Water dripped from the pipes onto the dirty bed and toilet behind me. The room I was held in was a series of what looked like six or eight cells in a block, but from my angle I couldn't tell how deep the room went. There was nothing inside the cells but a bed, an old toilet, and a metal stool. The floorboards creaked with footfalls overhead and soft murmurs of conversation being carried between two people—most likely Arturo and Miriam. No. She was hit with the crystal ball. Could she be awake and walking around after a blow like that? It was probably Marcus, *the dirty rat.*

I craned my neck to see further down the block, but I couldn't see anything but metal bars. I rocked back and forth, trying to free myself from the restraints, but the motion was too much for my fragile brain. My head felt like it weighed a million pounds. I'd brought Arturo back and the gold mark reflected that. It had connected across my chest now and probably reached down to my navel, maybe even past that. One more time, and that would be that. I'd cross over.

"Liz?" I called out to the other cells.

Her familiar dirty blonde hair was out of her bun, and it peeked between the bars of the cell diagonal to mine.

"Liz," I said. "Are you okay?"

She didn't answer me. Maybe she was knocked out still. I kicked a rock towards her cell. It hit the wall and came to rest by her feet.

"I'm sorry, Jacks," she mumbled.

"Why are you sorry?" I said. "You didn't do anything."

"I'm sorry I wasn't brave," she continued. "I'm sorry I didn't follow my gut that something was wrong with Marcus. I'm sorry I brought us here. I thought I could take care of you, but I'm not Dad. I'm not Mom. I failed you and now we're stuck here. This is all my fault."

"Stop that," I said. "You couldn't have known."

She hung her head and said something, but her voice was so faint the dripping water drowned out most of her words.

"What did you say?"

She sighed. "We should give them what they want. It's the only way out."

There was a groaning sound of someone trying to speak, but muffled, like they were gagged. I strained to listen. It was faint, but there was definitely another person in here with us.

"Do you hear that?" I said. "They've got someone else in here."

Liz rolled over and sat up. She walked to the edge of the cell and pressed her face against the bars. "I can see their shoes."

"Hello? Is someone there?" I said, a little louder than I dared.

A muffled answer came back, like whoever it was spoke through a gag or a busted lip. Even though it was strained, I knew that voice anywhere.

"Dad?" I said.

"Liz? Jacks?" Dad's weak voice called our names. "Is that you?"

My heart bloomed as I filled with every emotion I'd been wrestling with the past few days—relief, anger, worry, fear—and questions. So many questions. I could ask them all later because my dad was *alive*, and he had been here the whole time, trapped by Miriam.

"It is," I said. "It's us, Dad. *Oh my God*, I'm so glad you're okay!"

The door creaked open.

"Jennifer? Liz?" Marcus whispered in from the conjuring parlor.

I wasn't going to answer him. I bit down on my lip as my eyes burned. That jerk could go straight to hell.

"Go screw yourself," Liz said.

His footsteps fell across the concrete floor and over to my cell. "I'm sorry for what I said, Jennifer. Sorry to both of you. I know there's nothing I can do to make you both believe my apology, but there it is."

"Just stop," Liz said. "You don't get to apologize."

"I'm here because I'm setting you both free," Marcus said. "Miriam didn't tell me she planned on using your power to free my father, or that she planted haunted artifacts in people's houses to collect on the money. I thought those were just stupid rumors. I was so wrong."

He sounded genuinely upset by all that Miriam had done as he walked over to my cell. I looked away, unable to bring myself to look at the guy who had said such hurtful, disgusting things to me.

"If you use your gift one more time, you won't survive," he continued. "She knows that. That's what she meant by curing your gift. She's not going to help you. Arturo is going to use you both to open the Black Gate. Your body will fully cross over, and the Sparrow line will end. You will die."

It all sounded plausible, but I couldn't trust Marcus. I didn't care about anything that came out of his mouth—everything could be a lie.

"She made me believe Sparrows are the most destructive, selfish beings on the planet. I believed that. No matter what you've done, you were right when you said neither of you wanted to hurt anyone." He sighed. "I can't stand by and watch you both die."

"Just leave us alone," Liz said. "We don't need your help."

"Yes, you do." Keys jingled in his hands, and I heard the lock on my cell turn. "I don't care what you believe about me. Think what you like. I'm letting you all go, but just promise me you'll make all this up to Ashley. I don't think she'll ever forgive you, but you have to try."

I rolled my eyes. "Don't you think your father will notice if you let us go?"

"Don't listen to him, girls," Dad said and gave out a weak cough. "He's a liar, just like the rest of them. He doesn't want to help you."

"That's not true," Marcus said. "I hate my father as much as you do. I never wanted to see him alive again. I thought Miriam wanted to bring them here to keep people safe and prevent the Sparrows from crossing over by giving them a cure. She lied to me as much as she did to you. All she wanted was Arturo back."

He held his hand out to me. From between his fingers dangled Miriam's scarab necklace—the Obsidian necklace. He placed it around my neck and my whole body relaxed, relieved that it was finally mine. It would hide me from the spirits, protect me. They would never find me now. The power inside me roared louder than ever before, as if the necklace had multiplied it to the power of ten.

"Why are you giving this to me?" I said. "Why does it feel...so good?"

"To help hide you from the spirits," he said. "To protect you."

"Don't take it!" Dad yelled as much as his hoarse voice would allow. "That's not what it's for! It's not for protection—it's to open the Black Gate!"

Arturo smacked his son in the back of the head so hard Marcus fell forward into my cell. I hadn't even heard him enter the room.

"Shame on my boy giving the game away so soon." Arturo stood over his son's body, holding out another necklace. "You'll make quite the pair in Bonaventure tonight. I've got one for your sister too. You two are going to open the Black Gate and finally set everything right."

"And just what is the Black Gate," I said.

"Wouldn't you like to know?" he said, closing the door to my cell with a clang. "All good things to those who wait."

Arturo whistled as he sauntered over to Liz's cell. She screamed and kicked but the chair barely budged. The sound of her cries made the red and gold sparks in my arms ignite. If I was going to go out using the last of my power, fine, but I was going to protect my family when I did it.

Red lightning tore the restraints off my wrists. The cell door blew off its hinges and landed with a shattering clang. Footsteps creaked on the floorboards above our heads, hurrying to move towards the commotion. I had seconds. Arturo rushed out of Liz's cell. I sent a wave of light roaring into his body and he flew back into the cement wall with a giant crack. Arturo crumpled to the floor in a heap of black fabric. Blood pooled under his head.

"Leave," Marcus said. "Now. Before Miriam finds out what you did."

I hurried into Liz's cell, where she was also using the power of the Obsidian necklace to break herself free. "Not a smart idea on his part," she said, smirking. "Giving a weapon to the already powerful."

The Obsidian necklace gave off a sudden, velvety purple glow. I hadn't noticed mine was doing the same thing. My eyes widened. *Dad.*

"Dad!" I cried as I rushed over to his cell. "I'm getting you out!"

I gasped when I saw the man in the cell that was once my bright and happy father. Even my power, which was shining a moment ago, doused completely at the sight of him. He lay propped against the bed, both eyes so puffed up he could barely see. His purple lips were just as swollen as his eyes. The rest of his body was covered in dirt and old blood. Blood stains and the salt of old sweat hardened his plaid shirt and pants. His glasses sat on top of his head with the lens popped out of one frame. He smiled, so happy to see us, but the effort strained his already broken face.

"Jacks." His words hummed against his swollen lips. "Liz." I wrapped my arms around my father and sobbed into his shirt, not caring how bad he smelled, not caring how covered in blood he was. "I can't believe we found you. I can't believe you're alive."

Liz stood frozen behind us, expression blank, shaking. She was in shock.

I let go of Dad and took her hand. "Liz, it's okay. We'll get him to the hospital, but I need you to snap out of it. We have to hurry. Miriam is coming back."

Tears ran small trails down her cheeks as she turned to me. "Yeah. Sure."

"Daddy?" She kneeled and draped her arms over him and wept. Her back shook with her sobs.

"It's okay." His hands shook as he cradled our heads—from pain, lack of nourishment—I couldn't tell and didn't want to picture any of it. "I'm okay. You girls did so well. I tried to find your cure, but—"

The floorboards upstairs creaked.

"I think she's heard us," Marcus said. "You have to run."

"Where?" I said.

"Upstairs!" Marcus said. "Go through the Mirror Door. Tear a hole out the other side when you get upstairs. I'll hold her off."

"Go," Dad said, shoving me away from him, but the effort was so weak. "Leave me."

There came a huge groan from the other side of the cell block. Arturo was waking up.

Dad attempted to get to his feet. Liz caught him before he fell and wrapped his arm around her neck. "Come on, let's get out of here," she said.

I glanced at Arturo's unconscious body only to confirm he was still out cold before marching down the cell block. I hopped over him and out of our prison back into the parlor.

As she helped Dad limp around Arturo and out into the study, I approached the Mirror Door. The smooth, black surface gaped in front of me like a great mouth.

"Well that's just great," Liz said. "The only way out of this hellhole is fleeing to the one place that's worse than here. Besides, neither one of us knows how to rip open a door."

"You can do it together," Dad said. His voice was so weakly it broke my heart to hear his raspy voice. "Bring Summoning and Banishment together, two opposites and aim them at each other. In small bursts of great energy, it can rip a hole, or seal one, to the Other."

I shrugged. "It's worth a shot."

Liz rolled her eyes. "Fine, but I don't like the

idea of you using your powers. You're almost tapped out as it is. So long as it's a quick burst."

I nodded. "It will be. I can't afford to do anything else before we find a cure."

My hand sunk inside and touched a cool mist. I pushed my hand then the rest of my body through the cold, deep surface of the onyx mirror and disappeared inside.

20

The Mirror Door

I STEPPED OUT OF the mirror and into the haze of the Other. I didn't know where I expected to end up, but it wasn't right back where I started. Fog permeated Miriam's conjuring parlor and cast every vibrant color into ash. As I advanced deeper into the room, different bits came in and out of focus, slight changes between the parlor of the living and that of the Other. Each crystal glowed from the power inside, green or lavender or ruby. Bat wings, rat tails, fish heads, chicken feet, and other animal parts I could not name replaced the dangling herbs. The painting of the angel fighting a demon had become a demon surmounting the angel. Tarot cards lay across the once empty table in a crescent arc. They lay on a board with symbols and letters, lines meeting and spreading out in every direction, a great mandala. A pendulum with a silver chain lay by the deck. It was the one Marcus had used to find Liz.

This place wasn't just the reverse, it was purposeful, decorated. The door Mom and Amelia had created wasn't just a gateway—it was a place for spell work. This was how Miriam called the ghosts to her, how she sent them after me. Miriam had sent the Wraith that lit the match that truly got my power roaring, a beacon for all the undead to see. If it hadn't been for her, would the demon have found me at all?

Dad came through next, walking a little better, but still hobbling along. "Go on without me."

I draped his arm around my neck. "Not a chance."

Liz climbed through the mirror and did not stop to look at anything. "Let's go."

Someone climbed through after her. Marcus.

"Run!" I yelled.

"No!" he said. "Wait! I'm going to help you. I'll cover the mirror and lead Miriam away. It will buy you minutes. Use them wisely."

He climbed back out, and the exit went dark. He'd draped the silk over the mirror again. It was oddly effective at hiding the opening. On this side, it just looked like any other mirror.

"Why did he do that?" I said. "He helped us."

Liz took Dad's other arm and the other half of his weight. "Let's go. I don't want to stay in this place any longer than we have to. We can debate Marcus's motives later."

"Good point," I said.

We headed for the stairs, carrying Dad between us as best we could, but he was super heavy for such a dehydrated bookworm. We raced as fast as we could past the wall of photos. Their shiny surfaces winked as we raced along the hall and made it to the foot of the stairs. It was too narrow for us all to travel together.

"I'll take him," Liz said. "You go first."

I went to take the first step and hit a wall I could not see. I tumbled back into Liz and Dad, who caught me. Symbols glowed up the stairwell, a brilliant and angry magenta that shimmered like heat waves off a black top. I found my footing again and tried to push through the barrier. My fists slammed against an invisible wall.

"We can't go this way," he said. "Those symbols binds the demonic to this basement, and that includes you. You two are part...supernatural. It's how you can do what you do."

"What?" I said. "What do you mean 'part supernatural?'"

"I'll explain later," he said. "There's no time. We have to wipe the symbols clean. Let me. I'm the only one fully mortal."

He reached a tentative hand for the stairwell. Sparks flew, little stars of blue and white where he touched. He drew back, clutching his hand.

"Dad!" Liz and I yelled in unison.

"I'm all right," he said, though from the way he winced through his words, he clearly wasn't.

"Well, that was pointless," Liz said. "What do we do?"

"It seems it's blocking everyone down here that isn't a Blackwell," he said. "There's nothing we can do. We'll have to stand and fight."

The floorboards behind us creaked. Liz helped Dad as we dodged behind the door frame to hide. Liz hissed for me to stay down, get behind her. What emerged from the Mirror Door wasn't really a person at all. It was a cloud of a person, an outline, like a walking chalk drawing of a corpse in a crime scene—human in shape but not in detail. Inside the outline of his body, a green light flickered in his eyes as he ran towards us.

"What is that?" Liz said, raising her fist.

"I think it's Marcus," I said.

He flew past us down the hall and up the stairs, ran his hand along the wall and through every mark. One by one, the shields that kept us trapped winked out of existence. We didn't wait for Marcus to finish before we started climbing. Liz huffed up every step. It was grueling carrying Dad, but there was no way we'd ever leave him behind. I didn't want to think about what Miriam would do if she caught him.

The last symbol died at the top of the stairs. He'd done it. Marcus had really saved us. We were almost there. Marcus yelled something, but the words were lost to the space between our worlds.

He might as well have screamed underwater.

"I can't understand you." I said each word long and slow.

He waved his arms, crossed them in a show of warning. *Stop. Go back.*

"What?" I said, but he couldn't hear me in the land of the living. I was a ghost to him.

He stopped, raised one arm, and pointed directly behind me.

Arturo leaned on the rails at the foot of the stairs. He was alive, but in the Other his shadow outline appeared more like his original form. His waist coat fluttered around him. The skin on his face was so taut, every sharp point of his skull poked through—a dead man wearing a suit of old skin. He grinned, and even on the other side of the veil, I could tell his true eyes were red. Tar dripped down his beard and onto the stairs. I'd brought him back, but what I'd made live again wasn't really human—he looked like a demon.

"Where are you going, Sparrows?" he called, singing our names like a dark song.

"What is he?" I said. "How can he see us?"

"He's a soul eater," Dad said. "Didn't you read the end of the journal?"

"No!" I wailed. "It got water-logged."

I finally heard what Marcus was trying to say: *Run.*

"Go!" Liz yelled as she hoisted Dad up on her back. She'd always been the strong one, but I had no idea she had the strength to carry him.

"I said go!"

I did as I was told. I ran in front of her and took the stairs two at a time. My breath stalled and clunked in my lungs like gas in a sputtering engine. I hadn't had my inhaler in hours, had left it back at the hotel, and the lack of medicine was catching up with me. My hands hit the top steps.

"Jacks!" Liz screamed. "Look out!"

Hands scooped me up by my shoulders. Arturo's horrible, sharp face was up against mine. He grinned so wide his mouth showed all his teeth back to his molars.

"Come now, little Sparrows," he said with a voice as sick and horrible as his face. ***"Can't have you two running away before we have a chance to fulfill the prophecy."***

Marcus's formless shape came up the stairs. As he fled, he passed right through me. A cool sensation shook me like a wave in the ocean, carrying both of us in its strong current. I sighed into it and let the sea carry me. Marcus's emotions—his sense of desperation and fear and longing—I experienced them all in a breath. He had run straight through my soul, traveled through me like wind in a tunnel, and was gone. For a moment, he lingered in my chest—little sticky bits of warmth. His regret pierced an arrow through my heart. He didn't want to hurt me, never meant to hurt anyone—he was angry at himself, his family, at the curse. He didn't want to lose me too.

He wrestled with his father. He fought for me, held Arturo off so we could escape. My eyes welled.

"Come on," Liz said. "We have to move."

"But he's...I can't leave him."

"I know, I know," Dad said from atop Liz's back. "But we have to leave now."

It wasn't fair. My power was so useless. What good was it if I couldn't save someone from dying? Dad saw my face and smiled to comfort me, and I remembered his words.

If you will it, you can use your power for good, to help people.

Heat danced in my veins and my arms glowed red as we entered the furniture maze. The lacquer smell wasn't as ripe in the Other, but my nostrils still burned. I had no choice but to swallow the sour air down my raw throat. I ran after her, dodging through the furniture blur of white, brown, and blue. A sound grew above me, a cacophony of rumblings and threatening growls. Pieces of ash floated into a living abyss. So many ghosts rose and fell, I couldn't tell where one began, and another ended. Hundreds of demons crawled along the ceiling like angry bees in a broken hive. My breath caught in my throat.

Miriam had trapped them all here. She had bound them inside Blackwell Antiques to hunt the Sparrows down.

This had all been planned from the beginning, all the way back to the moment that ghost found me during volleyball practice. Once a ghost found me, once I awakened, Miriam would unleash all of her demons to come find me. He didn't come to Savannah for the Obsidian necklace— he came to force Miriam to break my curse. My heart sank. I couldn't stand how wrong I had been about my father, all my misguided rage. She had sent the Wraith, and in my fear to face what was inside of me, I had taken the bait. I had to make this right. I didn't want to be afraid anymore.

We found the clearing near the entrance again. Liz slid Dad off her back and heaved to catch her breath as she leaned on the fountain of dancing girls. "My back is toast."

"It's okay," Dad said. His eyes went wide when he saw me. "No, Jacks. No!"

Rivers of gold flowed beneath my arms. The burning sensation returned but not as hot as before. *Was this the power of the Obsidian necklace?* The tingling sensation flooded from my stomach and spread out across my chest. My arms and legs steadied as my vision cleared. I flexed my fingers and shook the last of the pain away from my body.

Liz gaped at me. "What is happening?"

"I feel...better," I said. "The burning is gone."

"Jennifer, don't use your power!" Dad said. "If you do, you'll be stuck here forever!"

He sounded so worried, but I had never felt calmer. Using my power with the necklace on was so different than without it. The light within me had focus. Wearing it, I knew no fear.

"I can tear them apart," I said. "It's okay. I can feel it. I can destroy them. Just like the Poltergeist."

The ceiling pulsed and boiled, grew from a churning lake to a storm at sea. Banshees and wraiths, poltergeists, and phantoms, all turned their eyes to me. Their piercing screeches of delight bounced off the walls in chorus. One wraith floated down, mouth wide, teeth gleaming. Volcanic waves left my hands, shot up and into its body, flooding light into its core. I crushed my hand into a fist. It popped, shattered into a million bits of ash and debris. They fell up and back into the mosh pit of demons.

"Damn!" Liz said. "That's incredible!"

"I know." I spread both hands and squeezed again, over, and over. Pop. Pop. *POP.* "It feels so good." They went out in rapid succession, bursting their innards up and out in firework blasts. I held my grip steady, but my hand shook with the force.

"Jacks, stop!" Dad grabbed my arm. "You're going to kill yourself!"

"I've never felt better in my whole damn life," I said and punched again, again, *again.* "If this is what keeps my family safe, I'm going to do it. If I'm going out, I will take every last one of these monsters with me." I became a living thunderstorm, a goddess of stars, a goddamn *superhero.*

The silvery light from Liz's chest sparked and erupted down from her heart to her fingertips.

"Come on!" Liz said. "I'm making the tear! We have to leave now!"

"Go! I've got this." I turned back to the ceiling. Above, the black lake stirred, the melted bits joining and reforming back to their original shape. *No. No it couldn't be happening.* The wraiths and poltergeists, they were reforming. They were regaining their shapes. The demons were too powerful. Everything I did, everything I just willed out of my body had done nothing at all. *Nothing.*

"Come on, Jacks!" Liz said. "Send a punch to me now!"

I did as she asked. I threw a wave of gold at her at the same time that she sent a punch soaring into the air. A brilliant, white sliver cut through the din. Light met light and burst our reality into pieces. Color flooded into our world. A circular disc hovered between us, just like in Castlebury's class. We'd done it. We'd made a tear out of the Other.

The broken pieces swirled and fused together, a living blob of nightmare faces, teeth, eyes, fingers, and claws. They bubbled beneath its surface, one expression melting into another. One eyeball became two, one mouth several. They kept ripping apart and restructuring, over and over, as if they could not find their original bodies or did not need them. They dripped down, down, closer.

"Come on," Liz held a hand out to Dad and helped him limp over to the tear. She helped him as together they re-entered the land of the living. They would be safe. They would live. *Good.* My arms radiated light, twin supernovas. Wave after wave of fire spilled from my mark and danced across the furniture as I sent a fresh wave through the teeming mass.

Someone walked towards me in the gray, an outline of a black Victorian dress.

"Jennifer!" Liz screamed as Miriam stepped out into the clearing, her eyes a brilliant ruby. I was helpless as my sister's outline fell to the floor. If I let go for one moment, all of the demons would escape through the hole we just created. She stepped through, leaving the Other.

"Stay away!" I said as my hands shook from the effort of bursting the demons.

"I don't need permission to take that which is mine," she said as she grabbed me by the hair and yanked back. She waved her hand under my nose and curling smoke filled my eyes, my nostrils, my mouth.

"Don't fight it, Sparrow," she said. "Sleep."

The smoke filled my brain as the light inside me snuffed out, and everything went dark.

21

Midnight

I WOKE TO THE unmistakable purr of a rumbling engine. Beneath me, the floor shook and vibrated. I was inside a trunk...or something bigger. *A van?* I blinked to adjust to the darkness, but there was no light for my eyes to focus on. I evaluated my arms and legs. My wrists were pinned behind my back, wound together with duct tape that gave a painful tug at my arm hair every time I moved. My legs were in the same state, but at least I had the jeans to protect me.

The brakes squeaked. I rolled until my back hit something soft. My fingers twisted around knotted strands of thick hair. *Please, for the love of everything above and below, let it be my sister. Let her be alive.* "Liz?" I called her name out into the black.

She groaned an acknowledgement back. "My head."

"You're okay!" I wanted to cry. "I thought when Miriam hit you…"

"No, I'm fine." The grunt that followed sounded anything but fine. "I'm just having the worst headache of my life. I'll get over it. How are you?"

"Tied up," I said. "Otherwise, okay. Where is Dad?"

"I don't know," she said. "Can you reach me? Maybe we can rip this tape off."

The car hit a speed bump and sent me rolling into Liz. "Sorry." I squirmed to get off her. "Whoever is driving this thing needs to get their license revoked."

"I think I hit someone else," she said. "Dad?"

There was no reply.

"Dad?" My voice trembled. "Dad, get up!"

"I think I found his face," Liz said. "I'm going to try and wake him. Don't worry. Just breathe. Dad is going to be okay."

I nodded even though she couldn't see me do it, a gesture more for me than anything else. I needed to calm myself down. He wasn't dead. He couldn't be dead. Everything was all right, was *going to be* all right.

"Dad?" There was a faint patting sound that could only be Liz trying to wake him. "Come on, Dad. Please. Wake up." Her voice broke as she trailed off into a whisper. "Please don't be dead."

"Liz?" His voice was weak and barely audible

over the hum of the van, but it was unmistakable. "Jacks? Are you there too?"

"Yes, Dad." I choked on the words. "We're here. We're okay. Are you?"

"Not really," Dad said. "Miriam stabbed me. It seems like someone bandaged up the wound, but I think I'm still losing a lot of blood. Where are we?"

"Not sure," Liz said. "Sounds like a van. How are we going to get out of here?"

"She's taking us to Bonaventure," Dad said. "She wants you to open the Black Gate."

"What is that?" I said. "The pages smudged. I'm so sorry. I never finished reading."

Dad swallowed hard. "It's the prophecy your mother and I found in New Orleans. Generations ago, there were two Beaulieu daughters born of a powerful demon coupling with a mortal mother. Their descendants are able to open the many gates of our reality—red, white, and black. The Black Gate is the gate belonging to Death. It is where those who cross over go when they die. It is the realm beyond the Other, the land of skeletons. To open it is to bring back any person who has died, no matter when, no matter where, no matter how."

No Sparrow could ever bring back someone who has crossed over.

The Black Gate—it was a way to do the impossible. What kind of power could you have if you could undo any death, for all of time?

"We are the children...of demons?" Liz's voice crumbled into despair.

"Yes," Dad said. "But that doesn't mean you can't do good. It's what I wanted to tell you. Just because you are the daughters of demons does not mean you two are evil. You have human blood running through your veins, a great capacity to do good."

So that's what Dad meant. All this time I thought that phrase had implied our powers themselves could do good, and in a strange way, he was right. I could help a ghost of a wronged person find another chance of living, and Liz could help those who wished to cross over enter the Black Gate. But neither of us could bring anyone back, not on our own. The balance of power made sense—it was equivalent exchange.

"We have to get out of here," Liz said, breathing heavily. "This is too much. This is all too much."

I couldn't think straight enough to plan. Whatever Miriam had filled my head with had done a number on me. My head swam like that time I walked into the girl's locker room before practice and found the place filled with smoke that stank rawer than skunk piss.

"Just stay calm," Dad said. "I'll think of something."

The breaks squealed as the van came to a stop. The keys jangled as someone cut the engine. There was a pull inside me, bigger than I had ever felt. It was like what I experienced back in Blackwell Antiques—the force of a hundred souls calling out to my power, only much, much bigger. I wanted to be wherever that place was. I wouldn't feel okay until I was standing at its center. The mark on my chest and arms burned.

The van door opened and slammed shut. Boots crunched on the gravel as the hook on the double doors at the back unlatched and opened. We were parked in a dimly lit area with lots of trees and tombstones. An obelisk towered in the center of a small clearing. Moonlight gently flooded the trunk, revealing Liz next to me. Her right eye had a big purple shiner.

Miriam climbed up into the back of the van and stood there, regarding us. "You're all awake. Good. Marcus, grab the Sparrows."

He stood behind her off to the side. When she called his name, he stepped out into the lamplight. A fresh cut ran down along his right cheek, clotted with brown blood. Similar cuts and purple bruises ran along his chest and neck, and there was a tear in the arm of his jean jacket. He looked like he had been slashed multiple times with a knife.

"No," he said. "I told you. I won't help you do this."

"Do you not want your father back?" Miriam said. "Is family worth less to you than a filthy demon Sparrow? They are dirty keys that unlock the door, nothing more."

"I said I won't." Marcus's voice boomed inside the van. The force of it shook my bones. "I'm not going to harm these girls or force them to open the Black Gate. That gate should never be opened."

She pivoted and pressed the salt knife against his neck. "Do it or I'll open your throat. I don't care if you are his son."

His son? Not hers? It was clear at this point from the way he addressed Miriam by her first name, that she was not his real grandmother, but was she also not his mother?

The door opened and closed on the passenger side.

"Marcus, my darling Miriam," Arturo's voice floated to us as his boots crunched across the gravel. "There's no need for such threats. The Black Door will call to them when we summon it, and then there's nothing they can do to resist. All these petty threats will serve no purpose, my dear." He came around the side of the van and gently took his wife by the chin. "If you so much as spill one drop of blood from my precious birds, or my wayward son, it's your blood that will flood the cemetery dirt. Do I make myself clear, *darling*?"

"Transparently." She removed the knife from my throat, but it nicked a bit of skin as she withdrew. A small trail of blood trickled down my neck to my collarbone as she pocketed the knife. "As you wish, *my love.*"

"Leave them in the truck," Arturo said, waving her away. "It won't take long to get the ritual going and then the gate will call to them all on its own." He paused. "On second thought...grab Jacob."

Miriam pocketed the knife and glared at Marcus to do what his father asked. He rolled his eyes and climbed into the truck to fetch Dad. I kicked and flopped my way towards my father, but Miriam was on me so fast I only had a chance to move once.

"Don't," she hissed, pointing the knife at me. "I'm not allowed to kill you, but this doesn't mean I'm not allowed to cause you significant pain. Lie still."

Marcus hoisted Dad up and out of the van with his hands still bound behind his back. Dad tumbled out, tripping and landing in a heap on the dirt and gravel.

"No!" I yelled, and Miriam smiled as she shut the double doors in my face. The lock clicked.

"So," Liz said. "What now? Can we finally use our powers and bust out?"

"Yes," I said. "Let's get out of here."

I rolled. I tried to flip over and find my footing. I shoved my leg up under me and pushed up until I was kneeling. A match sparked inside my chest and my power ignited. The flames beneath my skin danced. Fire engulfed my hands as the rope holding my wrists together burned away.

I swung my fist. Liz dove out of the way and my fist came cracking down against the side of the van. An atom bomb went off in my head as I was blown back and hit the floor of the van. The sound reverberated all the pebbles on the ground outside—they shook in a little twinkling rumble by the tires. Magenta light flooded the van for an instant and went out again.

"What just happened?" I said. "That looked like the same light as the stairwell."

"It probably was," Liz said. "They most likely put wards all over the place so we couldn't escape."

"Damn," I said, taking a seat next to her. "Now what do we do?"

"Help me get untied," she said and wriggled over to me until her butt hit my side.

I burned away her ropes with my fire and kept my glow steady so we could see. The flickering red and gold light illuminated Liz's face like a campfire, and her eyes softened as she looked at me.

"Jacks," she said. "It's going to be okay. We're going to get out of this."

"How?" I said. "They have Dad, we can't escape, and if I use my power one more time, I'm gone." I lifted up my pants leg to show her that the mark now reached down to my calves. I wanted to cry, but I had already cried so much the past few days my eyes had run out of tears.

She lifted up her shirt to show me her mark, which was at her stomach. It was like mine, but without the red-gold swirling colors of volcanic rock, gold leaves, and broken bits of ash. Her mark was the color of ice and snow, mist on a mountainside in an early morning, fog after a heavy day of silvery rain. She trembled as she put her shirt back down.

"It's spreading," she said. "I'm sorry I didn't tell you. I didn't want you to worry."

The van doors slid open again, this time revealing Arturo. He had donned a top hat and smoothed his brow, and his snake-and-bird embroidered black cloak appeared more lavish than ever.

"Time to go, little Sparrows," he said. "Time to open the Black Gate."

22

The Black Gate

THE DOORS BEHIND ARTURO opened to reveal an enormous graveyard, so large it was split by several roads. Statues of children with moss over their blank eyes and porcelain cheeks regarded us as we passed. Small fences guarded mausoleums that seemed more like miniature brick temples than tombs. The variety of graves seemed to stretch for a mile in every direction. The Blackwells had parked their van on a road alongside a clearing where a white stone obelisk of cut marble jutted out of the surrounding foliage in the center of the graveyard, the one obvious thing that was not like the others. It pointed at the gathering thunder sounded by thousands of lit candles of every size, shape, and color. A pink-purple glow danced along the base of the

Obelisk in the dirt where the grass did not grow. The strange light came from within, emanating from a tear in a jagged crack along the marble's smooth surface.

Miriam stood by at the base of a nearby tree alongside Marcus and Dad, who sat bound to the trunk with layers of rope. She had her arms crossed and looked so angry she could spit.

"Come along, Sparrows," Arturo said. "We ain't got all night."

He blew dust in our faces and my head swam again with that familiar wooziness. I didn't know what substance he had used, but it made the entire world spin and forced my legs to move all on their own. I stood up and climbed out of the van, shambling like a zombie where he wanted me to go. The power was still there, glowing like a candle at the end of its wick, but I felt no desire to use it against him. He beckoned Liz to join me and made her climb out of the van.

The light.

I couldn't stop staring at that light inside the obelisk. I wanted to be in it, live inside it, like longing for the warmth of the sun on your skin after a long, frigid winter. I walked towards it, couldn't help myself. I needed to be wherever that pink light was.

Something to the right caught my eye. A blue glow moved through the headstones, making its way towards us. It was joined by another, and another. More blue lights formed, grouped, and approached us at a steady pace. The temperature in the cemetery dropped as the little hairs on my bare arms pricked. I was able to turn my head in the other direction, but there were more orbs that way too. Hundreds of little blue lights hovered around the obelisk, so great in number, they obscured most of Bonaventure from view. The little balls grew, lengthened, stretched out into clothing. They formed hoop skirts and trousers, overalls and tattered gowns, flapper dresses and bell bottoms. The orbs formed features, shaping into noses, ears, eyes, and hair until hundreds of orbs became hundreds of people surrounding the obelisk as if in prayer.

Arturo raised his hands to greet them. "You're all here. How wonderful. We can begin." His voice boomed across the graveyard, but it felt as if he were speaking across the centuries. "Spirits, your time has come! Finally, you may cross the threshold. No more shall the gates belong only to the judgmental spirit Death. No more shall you be locked out, banished, cursed to haunt until you have paid your penance. Tonight, we force open the gate. Tonight, the Sparrow of Summoning and the Sparrow of Banishment will open the path to the land of eternal rest."

They hung on Arturo's every word, their opalescent faces full of hope. He gestured to them all with such love, as if they were his own children, but when he turned back to me, his eyes glowed red.

"Jennifer! Liz!" Dad called to us. "Don't do it! You can call on your gift! You can fight him!"

Arturo turned to him. "Miriam, would you kindly shut his godforsaken maw? He is breaking my concentration."

"Stay away from my daughters," Dad said. "Or I will—"

"What?" Arturo mocked. "I highly doubt you'll be doing much of anything. You see, you're not long for this world, whether by my hand or your own injuries. Besides, I get the distinct impression your daughters can take care of themselves. Since you were the one that led to my early and untimely demise, I'd say it's eye for an eye."

"Girls!" Dad said. "Resist! Call your power! You're more powerful than he is—"

His words were cut off as the handle of the salt knife crashed down on the back of his head. "That's enough," Miriam said. "They will do what they were made to do, and there will be no more interference from you."

Marcus grimaced and our eyes met. That green glow inside him. It was still there, but why? He had a gift too, but what exactly, I'd never been able to tell. Now, as I stood in Bonaventure unable to move, I could tell he had been bewitched by the same black powder. He stood unnaturally straight, arms at his sides, but in his face, there was a fight raging behind his eyes and that green fire was finally catching flame.

He held a hand out towards me. "Sparrow of

Summoning, I call to you."

My body moved on its own again and came to stand on the left side of the gate. Words floated up in my mind as my mouth spoke without my control. "I am the left side of the gate, and I stand to the east, the direction of the morning sun. I am all that is life-giving. I am a symbol of rebirth. Hear my voice and throw open the left gate." As I finished the ritual words, the pink light from the obelisk cracked at my feet and flooded the roots around where I stood.

Arturo held a hand out towards Liz. "Sparrow of Banishment, I call to you, now. Come to stand by your sister."

Her body moved on its own, and it shined like a silver star. "I am the right side of the gate, and I stand to the west, the direction of the setting sun. I am all that is life-ending. I am a symbol of rest and eternal death. Hear my voice and throw open the right gate." At the end of her ritual, more pink light flooded in from behind us.

"And now," he said, turning to us. "Swing the door wide and let the death knell be a toll in the sound of blood."

The ruffles of Miriam's billowing black skirts swished as she glided over to Arturo and handed him the salt knife with a deep bow. He took the knife, flipped it around, and sliced open my palm. My power faltered. Blood soaked the knife and spilled over. He took my hand and pushed my bloody palm against the obelisk. It rippled and widened. He flung me aside and reached for Liz, sliced her palm, and smeared her blood across the tear in the stone.

Arturo turned back to the spirits. *"Sit apertis portis mortis. Let the Gates of Death open."*

The wind picked up, blasting my hair back and forcing my gaze up to where the clouds spiraled into a funnel shape. Thunder rolled in the clouds overhead. A force outside of me, more powerful than anything I'd ever known, woke up my fire by force, let it rip up my body and burn through my mark. My gold was just as bright as Liz's silver. I reached for her hand and she reached for mine, and our powers touched at full volume. There was a percussive clap of air and the ground rumbled beneath our feet. Where the obelisk once stood, a black gate rose from the earth and grew above the trees. Wrought iron roses and coiled black spikes arched in ornate patterns to build the face of each double door. The ironwork fed on our power, sucking us both dry to stay in existence. The mark flooded down to my feet, taking the rest of my body. With a slow creak, the gates of the Black Door opened. I hung onto this world as long as I could, but my body was already breaking apart.

The second the doors opened, every blue spirit in Bonaventure flooded towards the gate. They dove in, pouring like water from an overflowing fountain down to the sea. My hair whipped around my face as the air whooshed around me from so many spirits trying to cross over.

Miriam left Marcus and Dad to rush over to Arturo's side, smiling wide. "You've done it! You've finally done it!" she said.

"Miriam." He swept her up into his arms. "You are remarkable."

He bent her back and cradled her head in the deepest kiss I'd ever seen. She wrapped her arms around him. I had to look away; their reunion was so physical and intense.

"How I missed you, Art," she said. "All these years, how I've longed to hold you in my arms again."

He let her go and kissed the back of Miriam's hand. "Now, to reunite the lost dead with those who loved her."

Her happy expression turned sour. "What do you mean?"

He let her go and approached the gate, parting the sea of ghosts with a wave of his salt knife. "The opening of the Black Gate means I can bring someone back—someone I've missed more than life itself."

Miriam balled her fists as her eyes watered. "You're not summoning *her,* are you?"

He grinned back at her. "It's now or never. I'm not letting my true love go. Thank you for all this time, my lovely Miriam, but you knew there was only ever a place in my heart for one, and I lost her seventeen years ago."

As they argued, my power surged, grew out

of my control. It spun up and out of me with all the pressure of a cork out a champagne bottle.

"Jennifer!" Marcus called out to me. Out of the corner of my eye, his body moved a little. "Fight it! Come on, you can do it. Don't let him control you."

"Don't interfere," Arturo said and sent a current of black smoke into Marcus's face. He flew backwards into a tree with a smack, but he didn't stay down. Green light caressed his hands, but it wasn't a Sparrow light, it was a darker color, deep as pine. It whispered instead of roared, crackled around his arms like two writhing snakes. "What is happening to me?" Marcus said.

"I can't...hold on." I closed my eyes. Ecstasy overwhelmed my every thought and feeling. I couldn't stop the thing inside me, the thing I was meant to be doing. I existed in that one moment, gazing at the hundreds of souls rushing out of the realm of the living to finally find their rest in the land of the dead. A calm wrapped my body in a warm blanket. The gold mark was all over me now and that warmth was fading fast.

"Jennifer!" Marcus's voice was so far away. Was he calling out to me in a dream?

The prophecy. I'd fulfilled it. I'm being pulled over. Everything turned gray. Liz. Was she being pulled over too? I couldn't see her. There was only a body made of silver light where she once stood. I didn't want to go somewhere she couldn't be. I didn't want to be without her.

"Amelia Beaulieu!" Arturo called out into the open maw of the Black Gate. "Come home!"

A delicate hand reached out of the misty door, pale freckled arms belonging to a woman with hair so fair it might as well have been made of snow. Her other hand held fast to a woman with red-brown freckles and equally red hair that curled around her waist. They stepped with bare feet out of the door of death and rejoined the living. I saw them—my mother, my aunt—and thought it impossible as the last of the heat left my body and the fire around my heart went cold.

23

Equivalent Exchange

"Jennifer."

Someone called my name with a voice I did not recognize, but it was as gentle and calm as the voice of my mother. I felt her near but could not tell which direction the voice came from. *Where am I?* I floated in a place without time or substance, unsure if it was deep inside me or out there among the gray. I opened my eyes. The woman with snow for hair placed both hands on my shoulders, a silver light emanating from her hands and around her eyes. She sighed and pushed that light into me, and it sank beneath my skin, impossibly both cold and hot at the same time.

The feeling of hot ice was fleeting and when it was over, I took a deep breath in and it was like being born again. I was flat on my back, arms and legs spread out, in the middle of a full colored Bonaventure. I wasn't in the Other, had not crossed over. I looked down at my hands. The mark was no longer there. My hands were mine again, a healthy normal color with freckles and fingernails and little hairs. *What happened? Where had the mark gone?*

The gentle lady with kind eyes smiled down at me. "Equivalent exchange," she said. "It's the hardest lesson my sister and I learned, to rid ourselves of our marks. We can push and pull our own power to equalize, for what is the opposite of summoning but banishment?"

Another face floated in next to hers, so familiar I instantly wept.

"Mom?" I said as my lower lip trembled.

"Yes," she said, kneeling beside me. She was wearing her favorite dress, the blue cotton one with the little flowers everywhere. "It's me. I've come home, my brave little Sparrow."

"What?" I said, throwing my arms around her as my voice broke with emotion. "How?"

"I was finally pulled over, just like you." She squeezed me hard, but her voice was distant. "I didn't have my sister to push back the mark. A demon came and broke into the house because one of the stones on the property had been knocked over. I died trying to kill it. Now I must save your sister."

She left me and kneeled beside Liz, who lay

only three feet away from me, her entire body shriveled and dull gray. The sight of her like that made my ribcage feel too tight.

She can't be gone.

She just can't.

I fell to my knees, clutching my chest. My mother put her hand on my shoulder and moved to rub my back in little circles like she used to.

"It will be okay," Mom said, and she floated away from me. I bit back tears as I watched her press her hands into Liz's. She closed her eyes and sighed as her golden light poured into Liz.

"What are you doing?" Arturo yelled and yanked at my mother's hair, pulling her back and away before she could complete the task. "You're not supposed to be here."

"Arturo, stop," Amelia said, getting to her feet. "Wherever I go, my sister goes with me."

Miriam grabbed the salt knife from her husband's distracted grip and struck Arturo in the back. Tears spilled down her cheeks, making trails with her thick mascara as it dribbled down to her chin. He screamed as he shuddered against where the salt knife had stabbed between his ribs and released my mother. The wind howled as Arturo turned, grabbed his once beloved wife, and yanked her back by the hair. "Jealousy will get you nowhere, Miriam," he said. "You will never be able to measure up to a Sparrow. You've always known that."

She squirmed away from him, but he held her

tight. "And I've always indulged your little trysts, but no more," she said.

The blue ghosts wailed as the ironwork creaked and snapped apart. *The doors.* With no powerful batteries to keep them open, there was nothing to stop the Black Gate from closing. A green light wavered between the other orbs and came rushing up behind Arturo and Miriam.

Marcus. His fists were electrified with the two snakes of light, which had formed into twin literal serpents—black bellied with emerald eyes. *How is he doing that? It looks an awful lot like...magic.*

"Dad!" Marcus cried as he thrust his fists at Arturo. "Don't hurt her!" The black snakes struck the back of his neck and spine. Arturo buckled, releasing Miriam as he fell face-first into the grass. Her skirt billowed around her as she fell delicately onto the patchy grass. She grabbed a fistful of dirt and watched it crumble between her fingers. As I watched her collect herself, an unexpected pity grew in my heart. She had loved a man who had only pretended to love her back, who had used her. No one deserved this.

"Mom!" Marcus rushed to her side.

"I am not your mother!" Miriam's face twisted with fury. "You're a filthy snake, just like your witch mother. You are not mine, and I've hated every moment I've had to act like it."

Her words punched me in the gut as everything slowed.

Marcus wasn't hers. Marcus was... a witch?

He gaped at the woman he had once believed to be his mother. His face fell with the sorrow of all he had done to please her, all the hours he'd spent at her disposal, all for the love of a woman who didn't even want to call him her own. "You're not my mother, are you?"

"No." She relished saying it as she pointed the bloody knife at him. "I don't have to pretend anymore, not now, not ever again. I'm done with both of you."

A blast of air knocked into us, the wind of a winter storm, pulling inward. The Gate—it was closing. I knew what to do, but I just had to gather the courage to do it. I ran up to Arturo and pushed, releasing a burst of my power into him as he fell. The blast knocked him back into the gate. He cried as he fell inside, and the fleshy mask he wore melted away to reveal his real one, the skeleton with barely enough skin to cover his bones.

"No!" Miriam's fury melted into fear, an instant realization that the man she both loved and hated would be lost to her forever. She cried and reached for him, only to be sucked inside the gate along with him. She clutched his legs as her body turned to ash. It was so disgusting I had to look away.

"I will be back," he said as his face melted like candle wax in the heat of the closing door. "There is no place you can hide, no place where I cannot find you. And I will send legions. Legions."

Arturo laughed, and with a flash of red eyes,

he and Miriam were gone. The doors shuddered as they clanged shut. Amelia, Mom, Marcus, and I stood in front of the Black Gate as little splits like cracks in a mirror ran up the length of the ironwork and broke. We ran, dodging pieces of debris as they slammed into the earth. The ground rumbled beneath our feet as the structure closed and came tumbling down. The last boom cascaded across the road, showering the path with dust and debris. By the time I had stopped running and turned around to see the damage, the Black Gate was gone.

Liz. We had never brought her all the way back over.

I wandered the debris, searching the rubble for any sign of her body. As the four of us scavenged the area, overturned rocks and broken branches, my hope dwindled.

"Don't worry," Mom said, putting a hand on my shoulder. "She's here, and if she's here, we can bring her back."

I stood at the entrance—now a pile of jagged black rock—and leaned against one of the massive boulders. "Where is Liz?" My voice broke as my chest heaved, struggling to find air. I couldn't image a life without her smile, her hugs, the funny way her smile was a little crooked on one side. I wished I had told her how much I loved her, how much she meant to me, but I never could again.

"I found her!" Marcus said.

Mom left me and rushed over to him. Marcus

pulled a piece of rubble off her silvery body. Mom kneeled beside the body of her eldest daughter and touched her, flooding Liz with her golden light. Air sighed into the silver lump and it stretched out, formed flesh and hair and fingers and toes. She took her first breath in and I knew what she must be feeling, but I tackled her anyway.

"Oh God, Liz," I said, racing over to her. "You're okay. You're really okay."

Liz sat up and I tackled her. She patted my head as I cried, and kept assuring me she was fine, but I'd never let go of her again. I'd never known relief like this, been so overwhelmed with emotion. I'd gotten my father, my mother, and my sister back all in one day. I couldn't believe with all the bad, something good could happen. Mom took us both in her arms and cried as Amelia and Marcus watched.

"She was always cruel," Amelia said. "I'm sorry for what she said when she died, about not loving you."

"I never knew," he said. "But I guess, in a way, I always did. She never let me call her mother. She always insisted I refer to her as grandmother, as if being my mother was a dirty word. Now I know why."

She nodded. "Miriam could not carry children after eating so many souls to prolong her life, an unfortunate side effect. Loving your father was never a healthy love, always a monstrous love. I learned that too late. Just because you loved a monstrous person, it doesn't make you a monster."

"What will I do?" he said, his voice so far away. "Where will I go? I have no one, and everything I was taught to believe is a lie. I don't know who my real mother is."

"That isn't true," Amelia said with a gentle smile. "You are not alone. You have us, and you will stay with us. We can help you find her."

Marcus smiled a little. "That would be good."

I sat listening as I held my own mother and knew what that must have meant to him, after all this anger, after all this time.

I pulled away from Mom and Liz. "We should check on Dad."

Liz, Mom, and I got up and walked over to the tree where they had tied him up. As I got closer, a hand went over my mouth. He wasn't moving. All the color was gone from his face. His skin had become pallid, a lifeless shade of gray. So much blood had gushed out of that blow Miriam had given him to the back of the neck.

Liz kneeled beside him. "Dad?" She shook him hard, harder. He remained unresponsive as her requests dissolved into sobs.

"Dad." My hands shook as I reached for him and took his hand in mine. It was so cold. "I'm so sorry.

"But he's not gone," Liz wailed. "He can't be. He was there and alive. We were here and he can't be dead!"

Mom took my sister and pulled her away from

my father's body. I floated through the motion of stepping away from Dad, not feeling anything at all. It was impossible. He couldn't be dead. Couldn't be. He was here, twenty minutes ago. He was still alive. He was just sleeping. He was just—

Mom kneeled beside Dad and touched his face with her hand. Gold light flooded into him. We all waited with a breathless anticipation—Liz, Marcus, Amelia, and me. I don't know how long we stood there before Mom let go. Her body crumbled, shaking with the beginnings of a sob, that's when I knew. That's when I dropped to my knees and didn't get back up again for a long time.

. . . . .

The sun was up by the time we were finished burying Dad. We found a shovel leaning against one of the mausoleums and picked a spot facing the river, not caring if the people who ran Bonaventure would let us bury him here or not. He would have liked to look out at the river. I sat beside his grave and picked up a rock and threw it in. My eyes stung as I watched the little stone sink to the bottom of the slow-moving stream. I had cried so much the past few days they were all puffy and swollen now.

Liz sat down beside me. "He would have liked this spot."

"That's just what I was thinking too." I plucked a blade of grass and twirled it between my fingers, not wanting to feel much of anything at all.

She put her arm around me and pulled me close, understanding she didn't need to say anything. I glanced over my shoulder at Mom and Amelia, who were talking to Marcus about something important. It didn't feel like we'd won, not without Dad. He'd fully crossed over and bringing him back would mean opening the Black Gate again, potentially unleashing Arturo and Miriam. Still, I would find a way to bring Dad back to life again. It didn't matter how. I'd find one.

"Hey," Liz said. "I can tell you're thinking deep thoughts. About bringing Dad back, right?"

I nodded, but the motion was painful and slow.

"Well, count me in, chickadee," she said, rocking me. "If we can bring back Mom and Aunt Amelia, we can find a way to bring back Dad too. I know it."

"What are you two whispering about?" Mom said as she sat down on the patchy grass next to us.

"Bringing Dad back," Liz said.

Mom sighed. "I want that too. But to do that, we'd need to access the land of the Dead, where all those who have crossed over go, and that requires the Black Gate. There might be another way. If there is one, we'll find it...together."

Marcus walked over to join us. "There might be an answer, in the basement. Now that the antique shop is unmanned, we should probably go back there, make sure all of the haunted items are dispelled. Guard the Mirror Gate. I could use some help."

I looked up at him and managed to force a smile.

"I think that sounds like a great idea," Mom said, getting to her feet and dusting off the dirt. "If there is anyone who knows a way to get Jacob back, it's Arturo and Miriam, and all of their notes are ours now. No one is ever lost. All we have to do is find the right door, and the right keys."

I looked back at the river, feeling a little better than I had before. We were going to get Dad back. That much was certain. I'd spent so long feeling like I was drifting, like dying was the end of everything, but it's like they always said, death was only the beginning. I wiped my eyes and got to my feet, hugging my Mom, my sister, and my aunt. Together with Marcus, we walked back along the dusty roads of Bonaventure, and my heart felt lighter.

I had a family. With them by my side, I could do anything.

With them, I could be the Sparrow, now and always.

For the first time ever, I was okay with that.

The Blackwells

Arturo Blackwell

Miriam Blackwell

Marcus Blackwell

The Stranges

Emily Beaulieu

Jacob Strange

Amelia Beaulieu

Elizabeth Strange

Jennifer Strange

Emily told me the news today.

We're expecting our first child.

I can't believe it. We've lived so long in peace in this house, I guess it finally happened. We wanted to try, knew the risks bearing a child might bring, but we were determined to not live our lives in fear. We wanted children to pass part of ourselves on. Maybe they will do better than we ever could.

If it is a girl, I know she carries the risk of becoming a Sparrow. Emily and I agreed we would do everything in our power to keep her safe, to teach her to be strong in the face of fear, but wise to choose her path.

No one should spend their lives living in fear that one day the worst will come. The danger will always come. No one should carry that burden alone.

If we have a Sparrow, I want her to read this.

I want her to know me, who we are, how Emily and I came to be.

I don't want her to live one day thinking she is defined by her gift, to think she's been given a curse. We are more than the card life deals us, and we can choose what we do with what we've been given. Emily and I will show her how to use her gift to help people. I hope this journal will serve as a reminder of the greatest lesson of all—that with her family beside her, there's nothing she can't do.

   Jacob
   June 16, 2001

The End

Acknowledgments

"So, what other ideas have you got?"

Jennifer Strange popped into my head in the spring of my senior year at Western Carolina University. I was in a TV pilot writing class and had essentially pitched a show about a skeptic and a believer who solve supernatural cases and my wise professor told me to go to the library and check out a little show called *The X-Files*. The irony that my married name ended up becoming Scully is not lost on me. After a night overloading my brain on reading Alan Moore's *Watchmen* and re-reading Neil Gaiman, the concept for Jennifer Strange was born. At its heart, it's still a show about a skeptic and a believer, only that believer is a redhead who believes her terrible power can do good and that skeptic is one who needs to see it to believe it. This concept has seen a lot of iterations, been through ten years of revisions and retooling, and there are a lot of people to thank over that amount of time. I will try to keep it brief, but my friends know nothing I say is ever brief.

The first person I'm thanking is my husband, who has suffered more than anyone else during the many years I worked on this novel. Michael,

I would not be here had you not convinced me time and time again not to throw my book into a burning volcano. How can I ever repay you for all that you've done? How many hours you cooked dinner, played with the kids, stopped the cat from crawling on my computer? Thank you for everything. This novel wouldn't be here without you.

Tommy and Rachel, your mom loves you more than anything. I swear the novel is done now. I hope you read this and know you can do anything you want in this entire world.

Miriam Kriss, my wonderful agent who worked on this book through heart failure and memory loss with me. I can't believe I lucked out in getting to collaborate with you, my favorite cheerleader and brainstorming partner. I can't wait to write so many more weird books with you.

My editor John McIlveen, who convinced me this novel did not actually belong in the trash. I am so happy you bought it and helped me see I am a good writer after all. Thank you for helping me put this weird little book out in the universe despite all the hell you've been through this year.

Trisha Wooldridge, who helped me get this book over the finish line by asking so many questions and helping me believe in the book again. It was no small feat all the hours and revisions and time you put into this world with me. This book breathed again because of you.

Chris Golden, Jim Moore, and Charles

Rutledge—my brothers—thank you for all the times you've answered the phone when I've needed a brainstorming partner. Thank you for reading this book almost as much as I have, and for always being there for me. So many twists in this book are because of our long conversations. I love you all so much.

To Bracken MacLeod, for being there for me every time I've needed help, for listening to me spout the entire plot of Jennifer Strange during a car ride, for the incredible blurb that knocked my socks off, and for being the best among men. I'm so grateful to know people as wonderful and amazing as you and your family.

To Errick Nunnally for agreeing to take on this monster of an art project—you are incredible and amazing and I'm so sorry there is so much art. (He's an incredible writer and artist. Go buy his books. *All The Dead Men*. Go. Go buy it. Right now.)

To Dianne Buja for giving me the most amazing copy edit notes of my life! You truly got my voice, my book, and helped me tame this mess and turn it into something beautiful. I can't thank you enough.

To Jaime Levine, for giving me the best marketing and publishing advice of my life. I'm forever lucky to have you as a friend. I can't wait until I get to see you again and we can celebrate in person. You're getting so many hugs.

To Todd Keisling and Dyer Wilk, who helped

critique the cover of the book so many have loved. Thank you for all of your incredible design wisdom, for helping convince me I could actually design a book cover, and for being there for me through the difficulties of publishing my first book.

To Meaghan and Steven Gerard who toured me around Savannah and taught me all they knew to help me write the book. Ashley is named for you.

To my critique partners over the years—Jade Loren, Elizabeth Runnoe, Cayla Keenan, Andrew Munz, Juliana Brandt, Meghan Harker, and Kathleen Allen. You kept me going even when I didn't want to myself. I'm so lucky to work with such a talented crew. Thank you for all the handholding, the phone calls, the chats online, for convincing me not to toss this book into the ocean, and for how many times you read it. Thank you. I found my voice because of you.

My dear friends who have helped me, believed in me, or cheered me along the way: Jenn Menze, Amy Williams, Kat Zhang, Juliana Brandt, Andrea Judy, Amanda and Bill Gardner, Hillary Monahan, my Necon family, the Northbridge critique group, Paul Tremblay, Chuck Wendig, Delilah Dawson, Claire Legrand, Sarah Jude, Anna Rae Mercier, Ali Fisher, Michael and Shawn Rasmussen, Zig Zag Claybourne, Nikki Woolfolk, all of my agent siblings, everyone who ever commissioned me for art, and everyone else I didn't mention. Thank you for helping me along the way.

To my family, particularly my mom who will wander into this book and not know what happened or where she is but will leave it maybe having a new appreciation for horror. Thank you for all those hours you took me to the bookstore, for reading to me, for showing me the hidden worlds of books and was for being the first to tell me I could write. To my brother and sister, this book is about you and for you. I thought of you both the entire time I wrote it. To my Dad, who I look up to more than anyone. Thank you for all that you've done for me so I could be where I am today. I love you all.

To my husband's family, who have cheered me on, and I hope you will enjoy this book despite how many people I kill with violent deaths. In all seriousness, I would not be here without your love and support. Thank you for all the times you've been there for me and believed in and supported me. I love you all so very much.

Cat Scully
February 2020

About the author

CAT SCULLY IS BEST known for her world maps, which are featured in the *Brooklyn Brujas* trilogy by Zoraida Cordova, *Winterspell* by Claire Legrand, and *Give the Dark My Love* by Beth Revis. She works in video game development for the Deep End Games, designing interfaces for their next title. She loves Earl Grey tea, video games, *Evil Dead*, *Hellboy*, painting, horror movies, and plays the drums. She lives in Boston with her husband, two children, and her cat, Pumpkin. JENNIFER STRANGE is her first novel.

She is represented by Miriam Kriss of the Irene Goodman Literary Agency.

You can follow her online at catherinescully.com or on Instagram and Twitter at @CatMScully.

CPSIA information can be obtained
at www.ICGtesting.com
Printed in the USA
LVHW081640121020
668588LV00014B/234/J

CARMEL CLAY PUBLIC LIBRARY
3 1690 02243 1440

CARMEL CLAY PUBLIC LIBRARY
Renewal Line: (317) 814-3936
www.carmel.lib.in.us